Something Deadly on Desert Drive

Something Deadly on Desert Drive

An Accidental Detective Mystery

Kris Bock

TULE
PUBLISHING

Something Deadly on Desert Drive
Copyright© 2022 Kris Bock
Tule Publishing First Printing, June 2022

The Tule Publishing, Inc.

ALL RIGHTS RESERVED

First Publication by Tule Publishing 2022

Cover design by ebooklaunch

No part of this book may be used or reproduced in any manner whatsoever without written permission except in the case of brief quotations embodied in critical articles and reviews.

This is a work of fiction. Names, characters, places, and incidents are products of the author's imagination or are used fictitiously. Any resemblance to actual events, locales, organizations, or persons, living or dead, is entirely coincidental.

ISBN: 978-1-956387-99-5

Chapter One

"LOOKS LIKE WE'RE the last ones to arrive." Dad raised his hand to acknowledge his friend's wave.

I followed Dad to the diner table where his friends sat. They greeted me warmly. This was only the second time I'd joined Dad's twice-weekly coffee group in the month I'd been home. They were nice guys, but since I was living with my father again, I wanted to ensure he had a social life apart from me. This time, however, they had specifically requested my presence.

Which meant they wanted something.

I couldn't wait to find out what.

I'd gotten through my first week back home, after decades of traveling the world as a war correspondent, by solving a mystery at my mother's Alzheimer's care unit and putting away a killer. The next month had been filled with writing Associated Press articles about those events, and then longer magazine articles on the challenges of finding and paying for suitable care for elderly people, especially those with special needs. I'd hardly scratched the surface of the topic, but I'd done what I could for now. I was ready for a new mental challenge.

I already had enough of a physical one with PT and getting used to walking with a cane.

"Thanks for coming, Kate. We need your expert advice." Joe Washington and his wife had helped with the nursing home investigation. Joe wore his white hair trimmed close to his head, forming a handsome contrast to his dark skin.

"Glad to help," I said. "What's up?"

The four men looked at each other. Dad nodded to one of them. "You start, Clarence. You were the first to notice something wrong."

"We're worried about our friend, Larry," Clarence said. "His wife died last year, and he remarried in the spring. We have concerns about his new wife. She is very young, maybe your age."

While I chuckled at the thought of being "very young," I had no desire to get involved in someone's marriage, especially if his friends' disapproval was only due to the age difference or loyalty to the old wife.

Clarence pushed his glasses farther up his large nose. "She's loud and bossy, and her children are worse. They're in their twenties, and the son in particular is a layabout who doesn't even have a job. We believe they are all after Larry's money."

"Do you have any evidence to support that?" The older generations sometimes had a hard time understanding how tough the job market could be for millennials.

"I was Larry's CPA for many years. I've mostly retired, but I still handle taxes for a few friends."

An accountant. That might explain why Clarence wore a button-up, long-sleeved white shirt, while the other men wore polo shirts in various colors.

"At first, Larry seemed happy after he married Pamela," Clarence said. "They went on a month-long honeymoon that must have cost a fortune. After they returned, I reminded Larry to revise his will if he wanted to make sure his children got some of his money. He agreed he would. That was the last time he seemed happy."

The other men nodded.

"After that, he made excuses not to come to coffee," Joe said. "When he did come, he brought Pamela. We don't have a rule against bringing wives, but most of them are happy to get rid of us for a while."

"Does Pamela work?" I asked.

"Not since she married Larry," Clarence said.

Change could be hard on everyone. It was possible Pamela and Larry were enjoying their newlywed time together. Larry might have picked up on his friends' disapproval and resented it, so he didn't want to spend as much time with them. He might have brought Pamela hoping she'd make a good impression.

"He hasn't joined our coffee group in over two months," Dad said. "Pamela says he's getting dementia. She won't let him leave the house."

"That's tough." It was also another explanation for the change in Larry's behavior. I could feel sorry for these men who had lost their friend, but I might also feel sorry for the younger wife who found herself taking care of an elderly man with dementia after only a few months of marriage.

"I've offered to pick up Larry," Dad said. "I have some experience with memory patients, given your mother, and I'm sure we could handle Larry for an hour or two, but

Pamela refuses. She won't even let us visit at their house. She says Larry isn't up for visitors."

"That does seem strange," I said. "Maybe he's not comfortable with visitors."

That could happen if he was embarrassed about his symptoms, or if his dementia was the type and degree to cause anxiety and even paranoia around people he no longer recognized. Still, the men's concern made sense. I was trying to keep an open mind and even play devil's advocate for Pamela, but the journalist in me smelled a potential story. Pamela could be cutting off Larry from his support system.

"We know our group is going to get smaller over the years," Joe Washington said. "That's inevitable at our age. But Larry was fine six months ago, and now this?"

"It happens, I'm afraid. Still, some medicines can cause symptoms similar to dementia." I'd learned that doing research for my articles on elder care. "To start, a doctor should review Larry's medicine. Has he seen a specialist for the dementia?"

Clarence crossed his arms and sat back with a huff. "Who knows? Pamela claims she's getting him the best care, but she could be lying. He is completely at her mercy."

I pondered the situation. I'd witnessed plenty of examples of people doing terrible things to other people. The elderly and sick were victims more often than others. But this still could be nothing more than a group of old men resenting a friend being taken from them and fearing their own decline.

"I suppose his wife has a legal right to make decisions about his care," I said. "Does he have any children who could intervene? The doctors aren't going to give information to anyone else."

"He has a daughter in Minneapolis who stopped talking to him after he remarried," Clarence said. "His son lives overseas, Hong Kong I think, and doesn't get back very often."

We paused while the waitress came over to fill coffee cups. "Good morning, gentlemen." She glanced at me and did a double take. "And lady." I was the only woman in the group, and the only one under seventy, but with my hair going gray (or as I preferred to call it, silver) in a short pixie cut, my casual shorts and T-shirt, and my cane, I didn't stand out among four senior men.

"Food for anyone today?" the waitress asked. "A breakfast sandwich, muffin, scone?"

My stomach grumbled at that list, but Dad said, "Maybe in a few minutes, thanks."

Joe slid the basket of half-and-half and the sugar caddie into the center of the table and we started doctoring our coffee.

Speaking of doctoring, I turned to Arnold, a slender Asian man with wispy gray hair and glasses. "Aren't you a doctor?"

"I was an obstetrician, and I haven't practiced in ten years. I'm hardly the person to diagnose conditions affecting the memory, even if Pamela would let me see Larry, which she won't. Now if Floyd were here—but he's visiting family in Pennsylvania for another month."

"Why anyone would go to Pennsylvania for the winter and stay in Arizona for the summer I cannot understand,"

Clarence muttered.

"In Arizona, the four seasons are tolerable, hot, really hot, and are you kidding me?" Arnold said.

Clarence looked at me. "How do you find an Arizonan in a room full of people?"

"Huh?"

"You say, 'You won't believe how hot it was back home today.'"

"You want to talk about *hot*!" Arnold said on cue.

Dad shook his head and sighed. "Clarence and Arnold have been like this ever since they took a stand-up comedy class together."

"As long as their jokes aren't as old as they are," I said.

Arnold threw himself back in his chair and clutched his chest. "A hit, a very palpable hit!"

"Arnold is also in community theater," Joe said.

I smiled, but my thoughts were on Pamela. I could understand being protective of an ill spouse. As a younger wife, she might be embarrassed by her elderly husband's infirmity. But when someone was old and sick, keeping him away from his friends wasn't helpful. If one of those friends was a doctor, whatever kind, I'd see that as a potential source of advice. Arnold might not be able to diagnose or treat Larry, but he could help Pamela understand medical terminology and point her to the best specialists.

The question remained: Was she overprotective and perhaps making bad decisions, or was something more serious happening?

"I'm glad to help if I can," I said, "but I'm not sure how. You need to know if Larry is really suffering from memory problems, and if so, if he's getting the right treatments."

Joe leaned forward. "When you were investigating Sunshine Haven, you pretended to be writing a story so you could talk to the family members."

"I did write a story."

Granted, that hadn't necessarily been the plan when I interviewed people, but it wasn't completely false.

"I'm not sure that would work here," I added. "Last time, I interviewed two women who had recently lost their mothers. Those obituaries had been in the papers. No one even asked why I was writing the article or who it was for or how I got their names. If I knock on Pamela's door claiming to be a reporter, she'll have questions. If I say I heard her husband has dementia and I want to know how she's handling that, she could simply refuse to talk to me."

I finished my coffee. It did not provide a sudden jolt of inspiration. "I suppose if I'm Pamela's age, I could try to befriend her, but that's a long and roundabout way to get to Larry. It's hard to arrange a meeting with someone who rarely leaves home, and if she's isolating Larry against his will, she'll hardly invite me to her house. Even if I could get in to see Larry, I can't diagnose his condition."

We sat in discouraged silence for a minute.

Clarence sighed. "We are aware that we do not have legal options for interfering."

"We have to do something," Arnold said. "If not legal, then—" He broke off and grinned at the waitress. "Morning, Grace. You ready to leave your husband and run away with me?"

"No, but I will give you the senior discount. Today we

have pumpkin walnut scones, pecan pie muffins, and apple strudel muffins."

The waitress refilled our coffee cups and we ordered our baked goods.

Once she left, Arnold straightened and scanned the area around us. He leaned forward, and we all did the same. If anyone was watching, our behavior must have screamed "Secret plotting happening now!"

"If we have no legal options, we must consider a less legal option," Arnold whispered.

Clarence's gaze shifted nervously, but he didn't disagree. Joe made a murmur that might have been assent.

I looked at my father, hoping this was an elaborate prank, but he nodded. Oh boy. I knew returning to Arizona and living with my father while my leg healed after the bombing injury would bring some unusual challenges. I did not expect one of those challenges to be my father and his seventysomething cronies luring me into illegal activities.

"Did you have something in mind?" I asked.

"Know any hitmen? We could bump off Pamela." Clarence chuckled. "Kidding!"

I decided to ignore that. "The goal is to find out what's really happening with Larry and whether he needs intervention. First off, we need to know if the dementia diagnosis is correct."

"If we take Larry to a doctor, we can get a second opinion," Joe said. "They won't release medical records to his friends, but they wouldn't stop one of us from going in with him. It's not uncommon to bring along a family member or friend to take notes during a visit."

"I know a doctor who would help," Arnold said. "He normally has a waiting list for new patients, but he'll get Larry in if I explain."

"How soon?" Dad asked.

"I'll call and check."

He stepped away from the table to call. The waitress brought our food. I traded half of my scone for half of Dad's pecan pie muffin. Clarence switched his yogurt and fruit bowl for Arnold's breakfast sandwich.

Arnold returned. "He'll see Larry today, if we can bring him in at noon." He didn't even glance at Clarence as he switched their plates back.

I checked the time on my phone. 10:40 a.m. "Guess we'd better make a plan."

"Pamela won't let us take Larry," Dad said. "We have to do it without her knowledge."

"How are we going to get Larry out of the house?" I asked. "I find it hard to believe Pamela never leaves, but we don't have time to figure out her schedule. Do we lure her out?"

"Maybe we could sneak Larry out the back," Dad said. "I think they use the back patio a lot, or at least Larry and Betty did, so it was always unlocked during the day."

"How hard will it be to get back there?" I asked. I couldn't see anyone in this group, myself included, scrambling over tall fences.

"The back of his house looks out onto the golf course," Clarence said. "The back wall is only about eighteen inches high."

Arnold made a skeptical grunt. "Larry is halfway down

the fairway. That's a hike and someone is sure to notice us, either golfers or people in the other houses."

Clarence ran his hand over his steel-gray hair. "Yes, a handsome fellow like me stands out."

"Stands out like a mutt at a dog show," Arnold said.

"True enough. I'm like the best mix of breeds."

"Maybe we should drive over there and take a look," Joe said.

We finished our coffee and snacks and piled into two cars. I rode with Dad.

"Thanks for taking us seriously," he said.

"Sure. You really think something is wrong?"

I couldn't help but wonder if this was a ploy to keep me entertained. I was doing a lot better physically since the bombing that tore a chunk out of my left leg, but I wasn't ready to return to world travel or tracking down warlords and might never be. Using my journalism skills to ferret out problems close to home kept life interesting, but I didn't need Dad creating challenges purely for my benefit.

He didn't answer at first. Had I hit on the truth?

"I know it's hard to believe," Dad finally said. "But I couldn't forgive myself if something happened to Larry, and I'd ignored the problem. Too often, people dismiss complaints from old folks. It's easy for a younger person, an adult child, even a lawyer put in charge of someone at a nursing home, to take advantage. If the old person complains, people assume they're forgetful or paranoid or don't understand the situation."

That was a scary thought. Dad's mind was as sharp as ever, but did people look at him and dismiss him? With my mother's Alzheimer's, we had to make decisions on her behalf. She had Dad, my sister, and me looking out for her. But what about someone who didn't have that support? My research had turned up one case where lawyers appointed to administer a million-dollar estate blew through the money in under a year, and then the elderly patient had to go into a Medicaid home.

"We'll find out what's happening," I promised.

We drove into one of the planned communities that were everywhere in the greater Phoenix area, with a golf course and clubhouse up front and winding streets throughout, most named after trees. A few turns took us to Desert Drive. Dad pointed to one of the almost-identical stucco houses as he drove slowly past. "That's Larry's."

"That gate must lead to the backyard."

"I'm sure you're right." He drove down the block and parked at the corner. The other car pulled up behind us and we all got out.

"I forgot about the gate," Joe said. "That's easier. We can park a few houses down and sneak through the gate, along the side of the house. Let's see . . . That side of the house has the garage, a guest bedroom, and what used to be Betty's sewing room. I doubt anyone will notice us."

I pictured us all in a row, four senior men and me, creeping across the rocks and past the cacti in the front yard. Yeah, that wouldn't look suspicious at all. The street was empty now, but you never knew when someone would drive past or leave their house, and it wasn't like our group could quickly drop to the ground to hide behind the single bush in the yard.

"We shouldn't all go," I said. "Anyway, we need to get Pamela to the front of the house and keep her distracted there."

"Right," Joe said. "Kate, she doesn't know you. You can ring the bell and say you're doing a survey or something."

"Hmm. She might say she's not interested and close the door on me. It could take several minutes to find Larry, convince him to move, and get him outside. We need to keep her at the door." I paced a few steps down the sidewalk and back. "Besides, maybe we shouldn't let her see me. That way, if we wind up needing a plan B, I can still be a journalist or whatever."

"She'll turn any of us away," Clarence said. "She'll slam that door faster than my ex spends her alimony."

"She doesn't have to let you in," I pointed out. "It's better if she doesn't. I nominate you, Clarence."

"But what do I say?"

"You've already shown suspicion of her. Get into an argument. Lean on the door or the doorframe while you talk, so she can't close the door." I gestured at his cane, the kind with four little feet for extra stability. "Make it look like you can't stand without the support."

"Oh, I don't know. I'm not good at confrontation."

"You underestimate yourself," Arnold said.

"I'll do it," Dad said. "Lend me your cane, Clarence. I'll bet Pamela has no idea which of us uses a cane. She may not even recognize me, but I'll make sure she knows me after this."

"Great. Clarence can drive the getaway vehicle," I said. "Dad goes to the front door."

That left Joe, Arnold, and me. Would we need all three of us to get Larry out? I couldn't go alone, because Larry didn't know me. I didn't want Joe and Arnold to go without me, because I wanted to keep an eye on the situation. I could go with one of the men, but it might be helpful to have a third person to handle doors and act as a lookout while two people helped Larry. We didn't know his current physical condition.

"The rest of us will go around back," I said. "Joe can go first and scout out the yard, make sure no one is in back. Arnold and I will follow. Dad, give us a minute to get in position and then ring the doorbell."

"How long do you think you'll need to get Larry out?" he asked.

"Five minutes? That will seem like forever to you, but we may need every second."

We couldn't see the house well from where we were, but I pictured it in my mind. The front walk led up to an alcove. The front door was set at least five feet back in that alcove. No one at the front door could see the gate opening, but they might hear us if we tried to cross the rocky front yard, especially if Larry was confused and asking questions.

"We'll stop inside the gate on our way out," I said. "If you're still arguing, I'll call your phone. Make sure Pamela closes the door as you leave. Then we'll all head for the cars."

Dad pulled out his phone and tipped his head back so he could study the screen through the lower part of his trifocals. He tapped it a few times and stuck it in his pocket. "All right. I'll feel it vibrate."

"We used to have to pay good money for that kind of

thing," Clarence said.

"Clarence, turn the car around now," I said. "When we come out, pull up to the house next to Larry's. Stay out of sight of any of Pamela's windows."

"I'll give them the slip!" Clarence said. "We'll go on the lam. We'll peach that gold digger and put her in the big house with a pair of silver bracelets."

"You've been watching gangster movies again," Joe said.

"Right. I always wanted to be a lookout man."

"Concentrate, people. Everyone know the plan?" I looked at each of them. "Now, let's kidnap your friend."

Chapter Two

WE HEADED FOR Larry's house. At the corner of his yard, we paused and looked around. Across the street and two houses down, a woman using a walker came down her driveway.

"What do we do?" Arnold asked.

"Pretend we're having a conversation," I said.

"About what?"

"It doesn't matter, since she can't hear us."

"Oh." Arnold thought for a moment. "Hey, how hot is it in Arizona? So hot the cows are giving evaporated milk." He continued with a string of jokes that most Arizonans had probably heard before, but at least it passed the time.

The woman turned down the sidewalk and crept along at a turtle's pace. It probably took her two minutes to get to the block of mailboxes at the corner. It felt like an hour. She fished out her keys, unlocked the mailbox, got her mail, and headed back. Fortunately, the temperature was pleasant in early December. In summer, our shoes would have melted into the sidewalk during that wait.

Arnold finished his stand-up routine. Joe gestured at a saguaro cactus in the next yard and rambled about landscaping. Many of the cacti wore Santa hats to protect them from the cold night temperatures. I wanted to stick big googly eyes on them.

Finally the woman got back to her house and the door closed behind her. Our sighs of relief would have blown the leaves off the trees, had there been any.

"Okay, let's go," I said.

The garage jutted forward from the rest of the house, so we couldn't see the front door or any windows from our corner. Pamela could be anywhere, including the backyard, but we didn't have a good way to check or time to worry about it.

Joe led the way to the gate. He was tall enough to peek over it before he slipped into the narrow side yard. I nodded at Dad and followed Joe and Arnold.

The side yard was only six or eight feet wide between the house and the fence. Rolling garbage and recycling bins filled much of that space. I lingered as Joe and Arnold squeezed through. Joe stopped at the far edge of the house and peered around the corner. He looked back and held up an okay hand signal.

Dad's voice came from the front of the house. A fainter voice responded. It sounded like a woman. Of course, it could be a housecleaner and Pamela was in the backyard, but this whole plan depended on taking some crazy chances, so I waved Joe forward.

When I got to the back of the house, Joe had his face to the window, hands on either side shading his eyes. That was one way to make sure no one was watching us from inside—and to totally freak out anyone who was.

He stepped back. "I don't see anyone." He opened the

back door. Thank goodness we didn't have to pick a lock or break a window.

We entered a great room with a living area divided from the kitchen by a counter. The voices were louder, Dad's raised in complaint and a woman's snapping answers.

Joe crept across the empty living room and peeked through a door on the far side. He had to be within fifteen feet of Pamela in the foyer.

Joe turned back and shook his head. We met in the middle of the room. "Not in his office," Joe whispered.

"Maybe the bedroom." Arnold jerked his head toward a door opposite the kitchen.

"He'd better be," Joe whispered. "It's the only other room we can check without passing Pamela."

I wanted to race into that room—anything to get farther away from the homeowner who would be rightly furious if she found us—but I forced myself to wait while Joe and Arnold went first. A short hallway led to a large bedroom with a bathroom attached. Joe and Arnold hurried to the bed.

"Larry! Are you okay? Wake up."

Their anxious voices sounded loud. I could close the bedroom door, but if Pamela always left it open, that would look suspicious. At least the argument with Dad was getting louder and might drown us out.

Joe helped Larry out of bed. Larry wore flannel pajamas, which seemed unnecessary in central Arizona even in December, but at least we didn't have to get him dressed.

"Shoes." I pointed toward a pair of loafers by the dresser.

Arnold held on to the dresser in order to bend down and

reach the shoes. As he straightened, he turned to me. "We should grab all his medicine. This doctor will want to see what he's taking."

Oh boy. I hoped his medicine was in the bathroom medicine cabinet and not someplace else, like the kitchen. I ducked into the master bathroom and checked one medicine cabinet, then the other. The second one held rows of prescription medicine bottles and some over-the-counter drugs. Fortunately, I had my shoulder bag, or I'd be dropping pill bottles left and right.

We hoped to return Larry in an hour or so. If we were very lucky, Pamela would never know he'd been gone. That meant putting the medicine back in the same place. I didn't know if they had a system, and I didn't want to take time to study the array. I took a quick picture with my phone and then shoved all the medicines into my bag.

Joe and Arnold had Larry up. The poor guy seemed shaky and was murmuring questions. They escorted him toward a door that led directly outside from the bedroom. That was a bonus; we wouldn't have to go back through the living room. However, we still had to pass the windows along the back of the house.

I ducked back toward the interior bedroom doorway. Someone at the front of the house was coughing. A woman's voice snapped, "Fine. I'll get you a bottle of water and then I want you to go."

Dad must be struggling to delay her. I shook my head frantically at the other men. They froze with the back bedroom door open.

I peeked around the corner of the doorway as a woman

with red hair strode into the kitchen, grabbed a bottle of water from the fridge, and slammed the fridge door. She stormed out of view.

I waved the men to go and followed behind them. We wouldn't have much time to get past the windows.

Joe and Arnold escorted Larry, one of them on each side of him. They had to detour around the patio furniture to get across the yard. I mentally tried to move them faster. It didn't work.

I looked at the windows, but I couldn't see inside due to the glare. No option but to keep moving.

Whack. My cane caught on a jutting table leg and jerked out of my hand. I grabbed the edge of the table for balance. That's what I got for worrying about the house instead of paying attention to my feet. Now I had to get down to pick up the cane.

Had I seen movement inside the house as I went down? I couldn't say for sure, but it seemed safest to crawl on my hands and knees across the hard cement. Ouch. At least I was only dodging an angry homeowner and not militia with assault rifles.

At the corner of the house, I dragged myself up and glanced back. The door to the bedroom stood open a few inches. It must not have latched when I pushed it closed behind me. If Pamela noticed Larry's disappearance, she'd probably think he walked out that way on his own, which was fine. The only question was, would she step out to the back patio and notice the open door? Would it call attention to his escape sooner?

It wasn't worth trying to get back there to close it. I hurried after the men. Joe looked over the gate and waved. He went through with Larry shuffling behind him and Arnold in the rear. I followed them out.

Dad stood on the sidewalk, and Clarence pulled up in the car. We all darted glances at the house as they got Larry into the back seat.

I checked the time. "I have to get to a meeting. You don't need me at the doctor's office, right?"

Dad handed me his keys. "I'll let you know when we're done."

They'd have a tight squeeze with five, and the doctor probably wouldn't want all of them in the exam room, but I understood that Dad needed to be with his friend until they had answers. My shoulder bag was so full of medicine bottles that it was easier to leave the bag with Dad and take out the couple of things I'd need.

Our car was still parked down the street. I enjoyed the short walk. My damaged leg muscles loosened up with exercise, as long as I didn't overdo it. Using the cane felt natural now, so I didn't have to think about how to keep my rhythm, except when doing something unusual, such as dodging patio furniture with my attention elsewhere.

I stopped by the car and took several deep breaths, letting the adrenaline fade. I was meeting Mayor Todd Paradise, once one of the hottest guys in high school, and now a divorced father of two teenagers. We'd flirted a bit, but this was a business meeting. He wanted my help with a problem in the mayor's office.

I got in the car with a smile and headed to the café where he wanted to meet. Life in my hometown was turning out to be nearly as exciting as covering coups and earthquakes, and meetings here were more likely to come with excellent baked goods.

Chapter Three

I FOUND A parking spot near the café and met Todd out front. We had that moment where we weren't sure if we were going to hug, kiss cheeks, or shake hands, so we wound up doing none of those things.

"Take a walk with me?" His gaze dropped to my cane. "If you're up for it."

"Sounds good." Not that I felt the need to prove anything about my physical abilities to him. No, I simply needed to get more exercise.

If you can't lie to yourself, who can you lie to?

Our community was technically its own city, but the borders had disappeared into the greater Phoenix area. The street we were on had been part of the tiny downtown for decades, but most of the shops had changed in the thirty years I'd been gone. The intervening years had given me sun-damaged skin. In contrast, this street looked younger now with its fresh paint, hanging flower baskets, and banners attached to the light poles.

At the corner, we turned and quickly entered a residential neighborhood I'd never seen. Had this been farm fields before? No, too close to downtown. It had probably been older and smaller homes. Certainly these McMansions hadn't been here. They were the kind of oversize houses with three-car garages that all looked the same except one had a Kokopelli metal figure nailed above the garage and the next had a Zia sun symbol. Neither meant someone with Native heritage lived inside.

"This has changed," I said.

"Yeah. It's a problem."

"Aren't these people good taxpayers? Their property values must be high."

"There is that," Todd said. "The problem comes from not having enough low-income housing anymore. I don't want our entire community to be taken over by rich retirees. People have to work in the grocery stores, pump gas, clean these houses, maintain their yards. It's not fair to make people drive an hour to work for minimum wage. They ought to be able to live where they work."

"What can you do about it?" I wasn't being flippant. Despite my experience with world politics, I had very little idea of what a US mayor did or how the local laws helped or hindered. "Something about zoning laws?" I guessed.

"A big real estate developer keeps building these communities. He wants the city to give him huge tax breaks and take care of the infrastructure. He walks away with a fortune in his pocket. It drives up house prices for everyone, which may provide some extra money in property taxes, but it hurts local businesses and poorer homeowners. Some of his developments aren't full yet, and he still wants to build more."

"I guess it's a business model." I knew even less about real estate development, but wherever you went, people with money and power tended to want more money and power, and many of them were willing to screw over other people to get it.

"The city council is divided," Todd said. "The developer donated big bucks to get one of our newer members elected. That councilmember is pushing hard on behalf of the developer, and he's convinced a couple of the others to go along with him."

"Now that sounds like the politics I know." In the developing world, especially in war zones, international companies set aside substantial funds for kickbacks. "Do you think bribes are involved? Beyond the bribe of campaign donations?"

"I couldn't make an accusation like that."

His lack of words spoke loudly.

"I've been trying to hire you as a PR consultant," Todd said. "I was impressed by what you did for Sunshine Haven. I figured if you could make a nursing home look good after patients were murdered, you wouldn't have any trouble promoting the town."

"Okay." I wasn't sure what else to say. For the moment, I was on medical leave from my job and still had health insurance, but if I couldn't get back in the field, that job might not last. I didn't want Todd to feel he had to do me a favor, but he had a point—I was very good at what I did. As a journalist, I worked hard to be impartial, but that meant I knew how to recognize bias. I could certainly spin a story if I wanted.

Todd shoved his hands in the pockets of his khakis. "This councilmember is blocking me, and I suspect it's because of the developer. He says we don't need PR and shouldn't pay for it because the local paper covers our meetings. The local paper pays fifteen dollars per article. As you can imagine, they don't have a knowledgeable staff that sticks around for years. Anyway, an article in the paper is not the same thing. They have fewer than two thousand subscribers."

"Right." Not everyone read newspapers. If they did, they might get the *Arizona Central* or even a national paper such as the *Wall Street Journal* instead of our little paper. A PR consultant could publish news releases with the spin they wanted and find other ways to reach people, such as the city website, email announcements, or hosting special events.

"This guy who's putting up the roadblocks—what's his name?" I asked.

"Eric Konietzko."

I'd get him to spell that later, when I was sitting down and could take notes more easily.

"You think he's trying to keep me out so I won't say bad things about the developer?"

Todd shrugged. "Maybe he's simply trying to make me look bad. I suspect he'll run against me in the next election. I'd be tempted to let him have the job, except I'm afraid of the damage he'd do."

I stopped at the next corner and turned to Todd. I didn't want to walk much farther, or I'd be limping by the time I got back to the café, which would counteract my attempt to look fit and active. Besides that, I was tired of people asking for my help without knowing what they wanted.

"What exactly do you want me to do?"

Todd hesitated, his gaze searching my face. "That's the problem. I don't know what to say. I'm not sure it's ethical for me to ask you to investigate a political opponent. I'm not sure it's ethical for me to let someone get away with this, if something illegal is happening. And I can't pay you, or even promise you work in the future."

"I see."

"Do you have any advice? That's all I can really ask."

The sun highlighted his hair, showing threads of gray among the brown. His eyes looked troubled, but the lines at the corners came from smiling and laughing. When he was a boy, a lot of Todd's charm came from his enthusiasm and passion for justice, his belief we could make the world a better place. He'd now seen the challenges, the complications. He was worn down, discouraged, but still fighting.

I wanted to make sure life didn't knock down the rest of his spirit.

I took his arm and turned back the way we'd come. "I understand the situation. Let's get some lunch."

We dropped the subject of real estate development and bribes while we ate. I saw why Todd wanted our conversation to take place outside, since half a dozen people stopped by our table during the forty-five minutes we spent in the café. He paid for lunch, which seemed fair since he'd both issued the invitation and hinted that he wanted me to do him a favor.

Back in the car, I checked my phone. No message yet from Dad. I texted him that I was finished and then checked my email. My sister had forwarded a flyer about an upcoming yoga class. Although she was two years younger, Jen had stayed in Arizona to raise children and look after Mom and Dad, so she often fell into a nurturing role, with a dose of CEO/drill sergeant to back up her insistence that we do what was good for us.

Or maybe this was part of Jen trying to rediscover herself. She'd admitted to being unhappy, now that her kids were teenagers and needed her less. In my infinite wisdom, which was more of a wild guess when it came to family situations, I'd suggested devoting time to exploring her own interests. Since then, she'd dragged me to a "painting with wine" evening and was trying to talk me into a meditation retreat. She'd even suggested we train for a triathlon. Fortunately, I could tell her my physical therapist wouldn't recommend that for at least another six months.

Yoga, on the other hand, might be good for me. Nothing too acrobatic, but stretching would help. Still, I didn't want to give in too easily. Jen enjoyed talking me into things, so I might as well give her that pleasure. I ignored the message and caught up on a few business emails.

My phone buzzed with a text. Dad said they were done and would head back to Larry's house. I started in that direction to meet them and help get Larry back inside. It wasn't that I didn't trust the men to handle things without me. Any one of them had more experience than I did when it came to both aging and doctor visits. I couldn't even claim I was faster and fitter due to my relative youth.

Apparently, I just liked to meddle.

I drove slowly past Larry's house but didn't see any activity. I parked down at the corner. When the other car pulled up ten minutes later, I crammed a hiking hat on my head for sun protection and got out to meet them.

Dad crossed to me, scowling. "We were right. At least, probably. This doctor isn't convinced Larry has dementia. It seems more like he's sedated. He fell asleep on the way there and on the way back and hardly kept awake in the exam room. Pamela has a prescription for muscle relaxants. If she gave Larry enough of that, it would explain his symptoms. It's a good thing you brought her medicines as well."

Yeah, I totally did that on purpose.

"What do we do now?" I asked.

"The doctor called Adult Protective Services. They should be here later this afternoon. Until then, we return Larry to his house."

He studied his friend, who was holding on to the car as if he could barely keep himself upright.

"I don't like to put him back there, even for a few hours." Dad sighed. "But we're already in a sketchy legal situation, and we want them to find him sedated in Pamela's care."

"How do we get Larry back there?" Joe ran a hand over his head. "We can't expect Pamela to stay at the door talking to Isaac again."

"I'll take Larry to the front door," I said. "I'll say I found him wandering. That will save the hassle of trying to get him in the back, and it won't matter if Pamela has already noticed his absence. Plus, I'll meet Pamela and she may feel she owes me."

It would be natural for someone who found a dementia patient wandering the streets to check back in a day or two to make sure he was all right. Pamela would be angry about

Adult Protective Services interfering. Maybe I could get her to reveal something. Getting Larry away from her was the most important immediate step, but what if she fought that in court? Could we prove she'd intentionally overmedicated him? What if we got Larry away, and she went on to pull the same stunt with someone else? This wouldn't be over until we took care of Pamela once and for all.

"Okay." Dad passed me my shoulder bag.

I went up to Larry and smiled.

He squinted, looking confused. "Do I know you?"

"No, we've never met." Sneaking him out the back of the house didn't count, and I didn't want him to think about that. More specifically, I didn't want him to mention it to Pamela or Adult Protective Services.

"This is Kate," Joe said. "She'll walk you home."

I took Larry's arm. Maybe it wasn't the best idea, me with my cane trying to help someone so doped up he could hardly walk straight. Still, we managed to shuffle down the block.

"I'm going home?" Larry said.

"Yes."

"Pamela will be mad. I'm not allowed to leave the house."

"Everything will be fine. You only stepped outside for a minute."

"I don't like when we fight. It's easier to do what she says." His words slurred. "I'm so tired."

"That's right. You'll go in and take a nap. Tell her you're tired and need to sleep. Don't say anything else. You're tired and need to sleep."

I wanted to let him know we were fighting for him, that he wouldn't have to do what Pamela said much longer, but in his sleepy confusion, he might say the wrong thing. Better if he forgot all about his friends' arrival and the doctor visit.

"Take a long nap and don't worry about anything."

"I don't want to sleep all the time," Larry said. "But I'm so tired."

I patted his arm. "I know. Things will be okay."

We went up the driveway. I had Larry hanging on to one arm. He outweighed me by at least fifty pounds, and my leg trembled from the extra weight as I tried to prop him up. My other hand held my cane. I imagined trying to ring the doorbell and both of us winding up in a heap on the ground.

I paused outside the alcove in front of the door. "You hold on here for a minute." I helped transfer his hands to the corner of the garage. When I was sure he was steady enough, I took the last few steps to the door.

I rang the doorbell and waited. No one answered. After about a minute, I rang again and knocked in case the doorbell wasn't working.

Still no answer. Pamela must be out, probably looking for Larry.

Larry was wobbling. I didn't want to wait around, possibly for an hour or more, with nowhere to sit in the front yard. If I'd really found Larry wandering, the natural response would be to call the police. In fact, if he didn't have ID on him—and it was hard to believe he'd been carrying it in his flannel pajamas—how would I explain knowing where to take him? Should've thought of that sooner. My mind, like my leg, still wasn't working as well as it had before my injury.

Or else my mind wasn't working as well because I was aging and hitting perimenopause, but I preferred the injury excuse. Injuries could heal.

I could claim Larry told me his address, but if Pamela came back with the police or other official help, I'd rather not answer any questions where I'd have to lie. In addition, the other men needed to get out of there before Pamela came back, saw them, and suspected something.

New plan. "Come on, let's go around back." I could find another excuse to meet Pamela later.

I managed to get us turned around and over to the gate. I scanned the street. No Pamela in sight.

Once inside the gate, I had to turn sideways to keep a hold of Larry and squeeze past the garbage and recycling bins. It probably took five minutes to get all the way around the house. At least I didn't hear a car pulling up or the garage door opening.

I took Larry through the door that led directly into the bedroom. I got him to the bed, sat him down, and took off his shoes.

"Go to sleep," I whispered. When Pamela returned and found him here, maybe she wouldn't bother waking him up to get an explanation. I helped lift his legs into bed. I wound up on my knees, but I finally got him settled.

Whew. Thank goodness this was almost over. I headed for the door.

Wait. I had to return all the medicine to the bathroom.

I sighed and turned back. It was tempting to shove everything into the medicine cabinet any which way, but I shouldn't leave evidence of our invasion. Speaking of which, my fingerprints were all over the bottles. I couldn't imagine why anyone would check, but knowing I shouldn't be there made me paranoid. I rubbed a dry washcloth over each bottle and used it to put them back on the shelf. I took the time to zoom in on the photo on my phone so I could put the bottles back in the same order.

Finally I closed the medicine cabinet, noticed I'd just left fingerprints on the mirror, and wiped them off. Larry was breathing heavily, making little "pooh" sounds with each exhale.

I let myself out the back, closed the door behind me and made sure it latched, and hurried around the house. The whole experience had taken maybe fifteen minutes and been about as stressful as trying to negotiate passage across insurgent territory.

By the time I got back to Dad and his friends, I was ready to collapse. All these short walks added up and my damaged quad muscle was trembling.

"Let's get out of here," I said. "We don't want Pamela to see us all here."

Dad looked toward the house. "I hate to leave until we know Larry's okay. If I sit in the car, I can watch the house. Pamela won't notice me."

"Maybe it should be someone who didn't just argue with her," I said.

"I'll do it." Clarence puffed out his chest. "The dame will never guess I'm a stool pigeon muscling in on her racket."

"I hope this gangster talk isn't going to turn into a running gag," I said.

"More like a limping gag, at best," Dad said.

Dad and I took Joe and Arnold back to the diner where their cars were parked.

By the time we got home, I needed to lie down with a pillow under my knee. I wasn't napping, merely "having a little rest," as Dad liked to say, shortly before he started snoring.

When I staggered back downstairs two hours later, Jen was on the couch with Harlequin, my parents' black and white cat, in her lap.

"Finally! Dad said I shouldn't disturb you."

I grunted. "Let me make some coffee."

"Dad started a pot of decaf when we heard you thumping around like a newborn giraffe trying to figure out how to walk."

I decided to take the "newborn giraffe" part as a compliment. It beat being called an elderly rhino.

I slumped onto the other end of the couch, swung my feet up, and yawned. Harlequin crawled out of Jen's lap and up my legs. He stopped just above my knees and meowed.

"I'm his favorite," I said.

Jen snorted. Harlequin stared at me until I grabbed the heating pad draped over the back of the couch and set it alongside my injured leg on low. I had a feeling it didn't matter how well I healed; I'd be using the heating pad as long as Harlequin and I lived in the same house. He stretched out on the other side of it and purred.

Jen turned toward me, her posture straight, her smile bright, and I was reminded of times when she'd tried to convince my parents a banana split made a well-balanced meal or that we should celebrate both Christmas and Hanukkah—with presents—even though we weren't really religious.

"We should go into business together," she said.

At least that made a change from weird new hobbies. It was only a matter of time before she suggested a pole dancing class or aerial yoga or ax throwing.

Actually, ax throwing sounded fun, as long as I didn't stumble and cut off my leg.

I yawned and rubbed my eyes. "What kind of business?"

"What you're already doing, investigating and stuff. Dad told me all about Larry Hodge. Clearly there is a need for people to look into situations like that, and need is just another name for a business opportunity."

"You want to start investigating? Or were you planning to handle the 'and stuff'?"

"I'll take care of the business end of things. I can build a website, get the word out about what you offer, schedule meetings, handle the billing. I can do research too. Believe me, I've nagged the kids through enough essays to know which are the reputable Internet sites."

"I'm sure you'd be great at all that, but I don't have enough work to need a partner. Actually, I haven't had any paid work so far when it comes to investigating crimes. I'm still mainly a journalist, you know."

"I can handle the business side of that as well, and you'll get paid investigative work if we set up a business and promote it."

I scratched behind Harlequin's ear and thought about how to answer. I didn't want to kill Jen's enthusiasm, but it wasn't as simple as she made it sound. If I wanted to get paid for investigating, I'd have to get a PI license. I didn't need one if I was simply meddling for free.

Jen grabbed a notebook from the table. "I've been making notes. A lot of the investigators around here have specialties: setting up security, doing background checks, finding missing persons, cybercrimes, uncovering affairs. There's even one who specializes in online dating. We need to decide your niche."

"I'm not about to spy on people having affairs." I had little interest in anyone's sex life except my own. "I wouldn't know how to do some of the other stuff."

"You can learn."

"Gee, thanks."

While I appreciated her confidence in me, I needed time to think everything over. Jen wasn't going to give me time, so what I really needed was a major interruption.

Dad's cell phone ringtone came from the next room. Maybe it would be Clarence with an update, and we could talk about that for a while. Anything to prevent Jen from talking me into a business partnership while I was too tired to argue.

Dad rushed into the room holding his phone. He stopped and stared at us, wide-eyed.

"What's wrong?" I asked.

"It's Larry. Pamela has been murdered!"

Talk about an interruption. Next time, I'd wish to win the lottery instead.

Chapter Four

We met Clarence and Arnold at the police station. The frazzled woman at the desk insisted that no, we couldn't see Larry, if any such person was even in the building, which she couldn't confirm, and no, she couldn't tell us anything more about Pamela's death, if any such person had actually died.

We obviously weren't going to get any more information there, but Clarence might get arrested if he didn't stop yelling, and Arnold acted like he was practicing a scene from *Hamlet*. Finally, with Dad and Jen's help, I dragged them outside.

This suburban police station was a far cry from the gritty ones in cop shows, let alone some of the places I'd visited in foreign countries. It was at one corner of a park, with other city buildings and a playground nearby. I led the way to some benches next to a swirly metal statue and sank onto one of them. The squeals of children drifted over from the playground. Meanwhile, we debated violent death.

Joe and Marty Washington hurried toward us from the parking lot. "What's happening? Where's Larry?" Joe asked.

"Did you get that counselor?" Dad asked.

"Yes, she's in there now," Joe said. "But what about—"

Too many people tried to talk at once. I raised my voice to cut through the chaos. "All right, now that we're all here, let's get the story straight. Clarence, you were watching the house. What did you see?"

He pushed his glasses up his nose. "I stayed in the car down the street. Nothing happened for quite a while. Finally, a car pulled into Larry's driveway and a woman got out."

"Pamela?"

"No. Someone else. I assumed she was from Adult Protective Services."

"What time was that?" I asked.

"Around four fifteen? Not later than four thirty."

I pulled my notebook out of my shoulder bag. "Tell us about the woman."

"I couldn't see her that well." He took off his glasses and polished them on a piece of fabric he pulled from his shirt pocket, as if that would help him see the woman better now. "She wasn't old. The way she moved, she was an adult but not too old."

So anywhere between twenty and sixty-plus. "Hair color?"

"Brown?" He squinted and nodded. "Light brown. That's how I knew it wasn't Pamela. She hurried around the car toward the house door."

I gave up on trying to get a better description of the woman. She'd probably be identified soon enough, if she reported Pamela's death. "Then what happened?"

"I kept watching. I couldn't see the front door because it's set back a bit, but I figured I'd see her bring Larry out. A few minutes later, I heard sirens, and a police car pulled up." Clarence looked around at his friends. "It was more than we expected, but I still thought it was Adult Protective Services coming to rescue Larry."

"We all would've assumed that," Joe said. "Go on."

"There isn't much else to tell. I figured it was okay with the police there, so I left. Oh, another police car drove past me as I was on the way out. I did think that was strange, but maybe if they'd announced it on the police radio, two cars headed over there at the same time."

Too bad Clarence hadn't waited around to see what happened next, but I couldn't blame him. In any case, he wouldn't learn a lot from down the street.

"Dad, tell us about the phone call."

He'd already covered that multiple times, with each of his friends when he called them and again when they arrived. Still, I wanted to get things down in order as clearly as we could.

"It was Larry. Calling from the police station."

"What did he say, as exactly as you can remember?"

"Let's see." Dad raised his gaze to the sky. "He said, 'Isaac? It's Larry. Something terrible has happened. Pamela is dead. They think I did it.'"

A visible shiver ran through Dad's body. We all felt the chill.

Joe slumped down on the next bench. "Going to have to pray over this one. We wanted something bad to happen to her. That's wrong."

Marty sat next to him and took his hand. "We'll pray it out."

"We didn't want her to die," I said firmly. "The only one at fault is the one who killed her."

"But if Larry . . ." Arnold trailed off and turned away.

"He wouldn't!" Dad said.

"He *couldn't.*" I needed to get them focused on the problem rather than worrying about their friend. "Think about it. This afternoon, Larry could barely walk without help. In a violent confrontation with a healthy woman twenty-five years younger, he'd be the one dead."

They considered that for a moment. I didn't believe it was *impossible* for Larry to kill Pamela, if he had a weapon or just got lucky in a fight. Still, it seemed unlikely, and his friends were near panic as it was.

"Then who?" Arnold asked.

Who, why, how? We needed to answer those questions.

I looked up at Dad. "Did Larry say anything else? Had the police arrested him?"

"I don't think so. He said they brought him in for questioning. But he seemed to think he was a suspect."

"As confused as he's been, he might be wrong about that," I said. "They might simply have wanted to find out what he knew."

"Maybe it wasn't even murder." Arnold clasped his hands under his chin and shifted his weight side to side. "Maybe she died of natural causes. Even a woman that age can have a heart attack or an aneurysm. Or an accident—a fall. The police would ask questions, but this may turn out to be nothing." He clapped Clarence on the shoulder, apparently ready to buy into that easy answer.

"I don't know." Dad raised a hand to his head, his fingers massaging his scalp as if they could free his thoughts. "When I asked what happened, Larry said, 'Someone killed her. But I didn't do it.' That sounds like murder."

"I suppose if she fell and hit her head, it could look like someone else hit her," Joe said. "I wouldn't feel so bad if it was a natural death. That sounds terrible, but you know what I mean. God's will, versus the hand of man."

Jen had been silent through most of this, lurking half hidden by the statue. Now she took a step closer. "That would make it easier on Larry and all of . . . us."

I suspected saying *us* instead of *you* was an attempt to integrate herself in the group, so we wouldn't keep her out of the drama like we had when investigating Sunshine Haven. In truth, she and Marty were the two people here who couldn't be linked to Larry's neighborhood on the afternoon of the death.

"Poor Larry." Clarence took off his glasses and pinched the bridge of his nose. "Everything he's been going through with Pamela, and now this."

Poor Pamela, I thought. She was the dead one. It was harder to feel sorry for someone who'd been sedating her elderly husband, but we hadn't even proven that yet. What if it was all a misunderstanding, and she'd been doing her best in a difficult situation?

I hoped we were right about her sedating Larry to get his money. Unfortunately, it would give the police more of a reason to suspect Larry, but none of us wanted to learn we'd wronged Pamela, maybe even somehow contributed to her death. I didn't see how our visit and her death could be connected yet, but the timing was troubling.

"We've done what we can for Larry for the moment." I turned to Joe. "Maybe the lawyer you called can learn more."

"I told her to call me as soon as she knew anything." Joe checked his phone and shoved it back in his pocket. "If they haven't arrested Larry, they don't have to read him his rights. He was so confused today, it will be easy for the police to push him around. All they have to do is prevent the lawyer from getting to him for a few hours, make her jump through some hoops while they tie Larry in knots, maybe even confuse him into confessing to something he didn't do."

"We can get that thrown out," Clarence said. "We have a doctor who saw him today and can testify to how confused Larry was."

"Two doctors." Arnold pointed to himself.

"You don't count." Clarence's jab was half-hearted.

"One, two, three, four . . ." Arnold trailed off, letting the joke fall flat.

"It's probably fine if Larry talks to them," I said. "He may not know anything about Pamela's death. If he knows someone else was in the house, that could give the police a clue . . ."

I trailed off. I'd been in the house twice. Joe and Arnold were there the first time. Dad had been at the front door. I'd wiped down the pill bottles, but we'd probably left other fingerprints and DNA evidence. That house had been crowded today.

"Do we tell the police what we know?" Joe asked. "What we did today?"

"I'm still confused about what exactly you did today," Jen said. Dad and I had filled her in a bit on our afternoon activities, but I couldn't blame her for feeling lost.

A big light came on above us with a slight buzz. Around the park, other lights popped on. The sky had turned the pale navy blue of dusk. A kid on a skateboard clattered past, bumping down the series of long steps.

"Don't lie to the police," I said. "If we tell the truth, all our stories agree with each other. That simplifies things. They'll probably find out the truth in the end anyway."

"But we kidnapped Larry." Arnold's voice rang out loudly. He ducked his head, and we all looked around. The kid with the skateboard might have glanced back at us, but no one else appeared to take any notice.

"Do not use that word when talking to the police." I dropped my voice. "Maybe what we did wasn't strictly legal, but we had good reasons behind it. All you did was take a friend to the doctor and return him home again. The police have better things to do than prosecute that."

"Should we go tell them?" Clarence asked. "The police, should we tell them everything now?"

Arnold made a sound of distress. "What about reporters?"

I decided not to take that personally. He was right—this would get covered in the press, and it would be quite a story, like *Grumpy Old Men* in a heist movie. I wasn't crazy about the attention either. I wanted to report the news, not be part of it.

"I've been reading old Perry Mason novels," Dad said. "If you believe those, the best thing to do is keep quiet and if they put Larry on trial, have his lawyer bring us all out to confuse the situation." He sank down next to me and sighed deeply. "Of course, if you believe those novels, doing that would somehow magically reveal the murderer during the trial too."

We didn't have anything to hide—not exactly—but we didn't have anything to gain by sharing our stories yet. I doubted the police would decide one of us, or all of us together, had murdered Pamela. Still, taking the time to sort through all our stories could distract them from the actual murderer, wasting precious time, and it wasn't unheard of for the police to find an early suspect and latch on to him or her to the exclusion of other leads.

"The police have their hands full," I said. "Let's not bother them yet."

"Isn't it illegal to conceal evidence of a crime?" Marty asked.

"We're not concealing evidence of a crime. Well, we're concealing evidence of kidnapping Larry, but we don't have any evidence in Pamela's murder." I rubbed my leg, considering the situation. "Chances are, they'll find out we were there today. If they talk to you, answer every question clearly and accurately."

"But remember, you have the right to ask for a lawyer too." Jen was now fully in our ragged circle. "If they try to bully or intimidate you, refuse to speak without a lawyer present."

I nodded to her. "Good advice. To some extent, as long as we all tell the truth, we support each other's stories."

Except I knew how poor memories could be, how the same people could remember events quite differently, how two people telling the honest truth could paint very different pictures of what happened.

"Go home tonight and write down what you can remember," I said. "Where everyone was, at what time. What witnesses we have. The woman with the walker. The doctor. Where in the house each of us went, in case they find fingerprints or something. We don't want them to get suspicious simply because Joe forgot to mention going to Larry's office, or Arnold doesn't tell them he handled Larry's shoes." I was nudging their memories, calling attention to things, but only to true things. No reason to feel bad about that.

Dad managed a weak smile. "If I'd known there would be a test, I would've taken notes."

I smiled back, hoping to comfort, but Dad had been at the front of the house, out of sight of the rest of us, and with Pamela. Would that come back to hurt him?

"Make notes about your afternoon as well," I told everyone. "We don't know when Pamela died. We last saw her alive at about eleven fifteen, when we were sneaking Larry out. I suppose it could've been any time after that."

"I never saw her," Arnold said.

"I didn't either, but I heard her arguing with Isaac," Joe said.

Arnold laid his fingers over his mouth. "I don't remember hearing anything."

"See, you need hearing aids," Joe said. "We've been saying that for years."

Pamela was alive at eleven fifteen. I hadn't seen or heard her when I helped Larry back inside, and she hadn't answered the door. I'd assumed she was out searching for Larry.

Was she already dead when Larry and I went in the house? I shivered.

When was that, anyway? Three or three thirty? I could check the time on the last emails I'd sent from the car.

I sighed. This was getting complicated, and it hadn't started out simple. "Does anyone have an alibi for the entire afternoon? Anyone who was never alone?"

"I was with this group, and then I played golf with another friend," Arnold said. "Oh, wait—I drove home alone, and I stopped at the grocery store for milk. I guess that's a gap in the alibi."

Everyone else had a similar story. I'd been by myself before and after meeting Todd. In the afternoon, Dad and I had both been in our house, but in separate rooms. I could not honestly claim I'd have noticed if he'd left for an hour, although I might claim it anyway.

"It is what it is." I usually hated that phrase, but I didn't have a better one for this situation. "Don't lie, don't leave anything out. Maybe it will never get to the point of the police checking our stories. If they do, lying will only make them suspicious."

"We need to know more about what happened," Dad said. "It's the only way we can help Larry."

No one questioned that we were going to help Larry. No one suggested leaving it to the police. I considered it, but I doubted that idea would go over well. Besides, I was caught up in this too. I wanted to know the truth. I'd only met Larry for a few minutes, and not at his best, but he was Dad's friend. He was a person who needed help. Regardless of his mental and physical state that day, the police always looked at spouses first in a murder. We'd hoped to free Larry from Pamela's control, but all our effort would prove useless if he wound up in prison or a mental institution.

"Okay." I glanced back over my notes, scanty as they were. "Who was the woman? It seems likely she discovered the body, since the police came so quickly afterward. Was she from Adult Protective Services? If so, how did she get in the house? Was the door open? Was Pamela out front? Did the woman look in a window?"

"How did Pamela die?" Joe added. "If she was shot—does anyone here own a gun?"

Clarence slowly raised his hand. "But I didn't shoot her."

Joe gave a bark of laughter. "Of course not. I only meant if they have a bullet, they'll be trying to match it to a gun. I'm sure your gun is where it's supposed to be and hasn't been fired recently."

Clarence looked a little pale. "I'll check as soon as I get home."

Everyone was getting paranoid. The likelihood of a killer stealing Clarence's gun to use on Pamela wasn't even worth considering.

"I don't know what else we can do until we find out more," I said. "We might have to wait for the lawyer, or tomorrow's newspaper. Maybe everyone should go home and make those notes."

Nobody moved.

"Or you could make your notes here," I said.

That got murmurs of assent.

"I have some blank paper in the car." Jen strode toward the parking lot. Leave it to a mother to be prepared for any eventuality. She probably had snacks too. Would I look like a jerk if I asked her for some? I didn't know when we'd get around to dinner.

Joe jumped like someone had poked him with a pin. I followed his gaze to see a plump Black woman in an emerald green pantsuit hurrying toward us from the police station.

"That's the lawyer," Joe said.

Chapter Five

"DIAMOND!" JOE HOPPED up and waved.

She bustled over and kissed Joe's cheek, then leaned down to kiss Marty.

Marty took one of the woman's hands in both of hers. "Did you see Larry? How is he?"

"They're taking him to the hospital for observation. I *think* I convinced them he's not faking his memory problems, or at least I scared them enough about the possibility that they're taking it seriously."

"What?" Clarence exclaimed. "Why would he fake being drugged or having dementia?"

Diamond turned and studied all of us. She didn't look intimidated by the crowd of strangers around her, merely curious.

Marty pushed to her feet. "I'm so sorry, my manners." She introduced us all. "Diamond is the niece of a friend from church. When this happened, we called her immediately."

"I'm not a criminal lawyer, but you won't need one unless Mr. Hodge is actually arrested." Diamond was the youngest of us by far, maybe thirty, but she carried herself with confidence. "In the meantime, I can make sure his rights are protected."

"Do you think he could be arrested?" Clarence asked.

Other voices rose with more questions. Diamond stood silently, smiling slightly with full lips painted burgundy, until the noise faded.

"I'm working on Mr. Hodge's behalf," she said. "I want to make that clear."

"Of course, that's why we called you—" Joe broke off. "Oh. You mean you might not tell us everything you know."

"I need to protect Mr. Hodge's interests. That said, I know you're his friends and you're worried." She put her briefcase on a bench and ran her finger along her hairline, first one side and then the other. If she was looking for stray hairs, she didn't find one out of place. If she was buying herself time to think, she kept us in rapt attention.

"Kate is an investigator." Joe gestured to me. "We've asked her to help Larry as well."

He'd called me an investigator instead of a journalist, which might lead Diamond to assume I was a PI. That probably wasn't an accident.

Diamond studied me. I tried to look smart and tough. Tough wasn't easy when you were five foot two and holding a cane between your knees, but maybe I could pull off smart.

"If you have questions, I'll see what I can answer," Diamond said.

I felt at a disadvantage with so many people standing around me, so I rose, despite the ache in my thigh. "Are they sure Pamela was murdered?"

"I don't think there's any doubt about that."

"How was she killed?"

"A blow to the head. If they know what hit her, they

aren't releasing that information yet. They'll probably keep it secret as long as possible."

Our group had shuffled into a tight circle around Diamond and me. The light from the lamppost shone down over us as twilight deepened into night.

"Did they find any sign of a forced entry?" I asked.

Diamond hesitated. Finally she said, "A window was broken. Some items seem to be missing. But I get the impression the police aren't convinced this was burglary. I'm not sure why."

I wasn't convinced either. The back door had been unlocked. A thief would have to be pretty stupid to break a window without even trying the doors first. Plus, why attempt a daytime burglary in a fifty-plus community where people were more likely to be home? Granted, some thieves were stupid.

On the other hand, someone who wanted to make a murder look like a break-in might have broken a window, even if they didn't need to get in that way.

I hadn't noticed any broken windows when I'd returned Larry to his house, and I'd been on three sides of the house. Did that mean the killer had arrived after Larry got back, or had the window been on the fourth side of the house? Or had I been too distracted to notice something that should have been obvious?

"Do you know which window it was?"

"No."

I tried to think of more questions she might answer. "Do you get the impression the police have any other theories?"

She studied Joe and Marty for a few seconds before answering. "I hate to say it, but I do think they suspect Mr. Hodge."

Several people burst out in defense of Larry.

Diamond held up both hands. "I'm on his side. The problem is, Mr. Hodge tells a very confused story about what happened this afternoon. He seems to have gaps in his memory."

"Pamela claimed he has dementia," I said. Maybe that would help him now.

"We might have to get his permission to release medical records," Diamond said. "Right now, we don't have proof of the dementia, and . . . well, I think the police suspect he's faking it, so he doesn't have to answer questions."

Oh boy. If it turned out Larry *didn't* have dementia, would that make the case against him look worse? Would they believe he'd faked his symptoms to have an alibi for the murder?

"The worst part is . . ." Diamond looked upward, as if seeking guidance from above. "I can't believe I'm telling you this." Her gaze dropped to us. "From my few minutes with Larry, he's not certain he didn't do it. He can't remember, and that scares him."

We were all silent for a minute. I couldn't imagine being in that situation. Knowing you were near a murder when it happened was bad enough. Worse that it was a family member, even one he might not have loved anymore. But not even knowing if you were responsible? Wondering if you might be?

I rubbed my arms. I hadn't bothered to grab a jacket on the way out of the house, and the temperature had dropped along with the sun.

"Can we see him?" Clarence asked.

Diamond turned toward him. "I'm not sure, but if the police keep an eye on him at the hospital, anything you say might be overheard."

"Can you make sure Larry gets a drug test?" I asked.

"I can." Diamond tapped her lower lip with one finger. "Any particular reason?"

"We believe Pamela was giving him a high dose of muscle relaxants to keep him sedated and unable to do much."

She bit her fingernail and then jerked her hand away and hid it behind her back. Maybe she had to work for that confident appearance.

"I can get the test done," she said. "I'm debating whether that would help or hurt him."

Clarence moved forward. "Wouldn't it explain his confusion and make it unlikely that he could have killed Pamela?"

"Not necessarily," Diamond said.

"If Pamela was drugging him, it gives him more of a motive." I might as well acknowledge that here, among the people who wanted to help him. "But if we can show how incapable he was today, that might help him."

"The police might think he did it in a half-asleep drugged zone," Diamond said. "Drugs are rarely used as an excuse for why someone *didn't* commit a crime. On the other hand, if we can't prove he didn't kill his wife, we might be able to prove he was incompetent at the time."

It was a risk either way. I guess I was still more of a journalist than a detective, because I wanted to know.

"I believe the truth is almost always the best answer," I

said. "The more we know, the more we can figure out what really happened."

"All right, I'll see that the hospital tests him. We might be able to keep that information from the police anyway, unless they get a subpoena for it. It's possible they've already asked for a drug test to be done, but given Larry's age, I wouldn't be surprised if they've assumed either he has dementia or is faking it and haven't even thought about drugs. It would help to know what drug he took."

"I can get you that info." The photo of all the medicine was on my phone. I didn't want to explain why I had it though.

She pulled a card out of her pocket and handed it to me. "Text me. I'll head to the hospital now. Call me if you find anything else that might help Larry." She said quick goodbyes to Joe and Marty and strode toward the parking lot, her heels tapping out a fading beat.

"She's so young," Arnold said.

Marty's chin went up. "Don't let that fool you. She's as smart as they come."

"Anyway," Joe said, "we needed someone fast, and she was available. For now, we simply need someone to make sure his rights are protected. If we're lucky, it will never come to defending Larry in court."

"Knock on wood." Clarence rapped on his temple. "What now? I don't want to sit around doing nothing."

"I'd like to say we can trust the police to find out the truth." Marty closed her eyes for a few seconds, her face strained. "But I don't believe that. I *hope* it, but I don't trust it."

Joe put his arm around his wife. "At least Larry's an old white man and not a young Black man."

She nodded. "Even so. I believe most police officers are honest and work hard. They still make mistakes. They still have biases. And they're always overworked. What if they decide the easy answer is to blame this on Larry, an old man who can't give them a clear story? Even if he doesn't go to prison, he might be sent to some kind of mental institution."

"Maybe they'll decide it was a break-in, blame it on an unknown stranger, and leave it at that," Arnold said.

"I'm not sure that's any better," Dad said. "People will always wonder, *Larry* might always wonder, if he did it. If he can't remember what happened today, he'll always have doubts about himself. I can't imagine living like that."

We had a moment of silent acknowledgment.

"Besides," Jen added, "that means a killer goes free."

"We have to solve this," Joe said. "We have to convince the police, and Larry, that he's innocent."

"Yes!" Jen grabbed my arm. "We're on a real case. This is going to be—" She broke off as she seemed to remember the seriousness of the situation. "We're going to see that justice is done."

"Justice," Arnold said. "We didn't save Larry today the way we'd hoped. We have to fix this."

Clarence put his hand on my shoulder. "We all heard about what you did at Sunshine Haven. You just have to do that again."

Great. I wanted to say, "Just because I pulled off a crazy stunt once doesn't mean I can repeat it," but that wouldn't improve the current mood.

Clarence squeezed my shoulder. "And now you have all of our help."

That did make a difference. For better or worse, I couldn't say.

I kept my snarky thoughts to myself. "Okay, we have some planning to do." That sounded positive, right? Planning conveyed the impression of productivity, even if it was really a time filler because you had no idea what to do.

"Is it time to make a list of suspects?" Jen asked. "I'll take notes."

"Oh, honey, you're shivering," Marty said to me. "Let's get out of here."

"We can meet at our house," Jen said. "I'll order takeout. What does everyone want? Pizza, Chinese, barbecue?"

We settled on Chinese and headed for the parking lot.

Dad walked next to me. "When I asked you to come with me this morning, I didn't think we'd be looking for another murderer."

I slipped my free arm through his. "These things happen. Well, maybe not to regular people, but I've met more than the average share of criminals, including killers. At least this time we have a lot of help and no reason to keep secrets from Jen or anyone else."

In the Sunshine Haven investigation, Dad had suggested getting help from his coffee group. That time, we'd limited it to Joe and Marty Washington. But we'd joked about an "old guys brigade" or my version of Sherlock Holmes's Baker Street Irregulars.

Dad patted my hand on his arm. "It looks like you have your Coffee Shop Irregulars on the case."

Chapter Six

THIS WAS THE way to investigate a crime: in my own home, with food, coffee, and comfortable chairs. We got everyone to write down their schedule for the day and whatever they remembered from our time in Larry's neighborhood. I wanted those records done before their memories faded or got more muddled. Plus, the work distracted the first arrivals.

Jen came in last, her arms full of bags. She set the bags on the counter and started pulling out containers.

Arnold stood and rubbed his stomach. "Looks good. What are *you* going to eat?"

Jen gestured at the array, enough to feed a dozen hungry teenagers. "All of this. What are *you* going to eat?"

"Hey, no fair. You stole my line!" Arnold cackled.

Clarence got up and grabbed both of Arnold's arms from behind. "I'll hold him back while everybody else fills a plate. He might look skinny, but he can put away the grub."

"You want a fortune cookie?" Arnold asked. "I bet it says you're going to get a punch in the nose."

I had to smile. Their spirits must be up, now that we were working to help Larry. This wasn't a game. We weren't doing community theater. But we had a group of friends quick to laugh together and ready to work together. In the eyes of mainstream society, Larry might not have much value. He was elderly, retired, and said to have dementia. But his friends wouldn't let him down.

With seven of us, we had to squeeze in around the table. Jen had a notepad ready beside her plate. She spoke between bites of her egg roll. "All right. Suspects—that's where we should start, right? Motive, means, opportunity." She nodded to me. Did she see this as an audition for a job as my office manager?

I opened my mouth to reply.

"Motive!" Clarence pounded his fist on the table. "Who benefits from Pamela's death and maybe Larry going to prison? Her children. They'll inherit."

"Will they?" Marty asked. "Larry would inherit from Pamela, unless she has a will that says otherwise."

"If Larry is arrested for the crime, he can't benefit from Pamela's death," Dad said. "That's the law, isn't it? I've heard that."

I frowned. "Some laws say criminals can't get money for telling or writing the story of their crimes. The money has to go to their victims." Journalists had to know that kind of thing. "That was overturned at the Supreme Court level, but some states still have laws to that effect. It wouldn't apply here though."

"Another rule prevents murderers from inheriting from their victim," Clarence said. "Believe it or not, these questions sometimes come up in accounting."

Jen was furiously taking notes. We had a lot of knowledge among us but probably a lot of misinformation as well. I'd want to check all these claims before trusting them. People often "knew" something because they'd seen it on a TV show. Plus, state laws varied.

"So if Pamela didn't have a will, killing her might get rid of both her and Larry so her kids could inherit," I said, "but only if they made it look like Larry committed the crime. Diamond said it looked like a break-in. Why fake a break-in if they wanted Larry to look guilty?"

We pondered for a moment.

"Maybe they didn't want to look too obvious?" Clarence said.

Marty took some chopsticks from the pile in the middle of the table. "Diamond said the police were skeptical about the break-in. The window might've been broken by accident at some earlier time." She tapped her chopsticks on her plate. "How would the police know if anything was missing? Pamela is dead, and Larry is too confused to know whether something should be there or not." She gave a last decisive tap with the chopsticks. "The break-in must be a red herring."

"It may be misleading, but the police had some reason to see a break-in." I pondered the idea of a broken window. "The window had to be more than cracked, if they thought someone got in that way. Broken glass would be a sign of a break-in, and a recent one, since thieves wouldn't clean up but homeowners would. The police might have other evidence they haven't shared. I don't think we can discount the break-in entirely."

"It could still be a trick," Clarence said. "Her kids might have realized it would be too obvious they were targeting

Larry if they didn't fake a break-in, so they killed Pamela, pretended to break into the house, and . . ." He slumped back. "No, I don't see why they'd do that to make Larry look guilty. With Larry so confused, they could probably put the murder weapon in his hand, call the police, and pretend they'd found him that way."

"What about Larry's children?" I asked. "You said they don't live around here, but we should check that they were where they're supposed to be."

Jen made a note. "Right. This way, they could get rid of the stepmother they didn't like, get their father put in jail or some kind of home, or at least get power of attorney, since he's not currently capable of taking care of his own business. Then they'd inherit everything of his."

Clarence frowned and shook his head. "I hate to say it, but that makes more sense than Pamela's kids. Larry was the one with the money, and her kids wouldn't inherit from him unless he left a will in their favor. I can't see him doing that. The only way for Pamela's kids to get the money would be if Larry died first, she inherited, and then she died or was incapacitated. They would've been better off killing Larry and making their mother look guilty or killing them both but making sure Pamela didn't die until after inheriting from Larry."

"That's so cold," Marty said. "I sure hope it wasn't one of Larry's kids. He's had enough heartbreak without that. He might not even want to get his mental faculties back if he has to see his child arrested for murder."

"Maybe they'll have alibis," I said. "Hopefully they were far away when this happened. They don't even have to account for gaps of an hour or two, like we do, if they're hundreds of miles away. All right, who else?"

We sat in silence for a minute.

"An actual burglar?" Dad said. "That would be the ideal answer for Larry in many ways, but I don't see how we'd find the person."

"No, the police have the advantage there," I said. "They can collect evidence at the crime scene. Check for fingerprints."

Fingerprints, including ours. The men were friends of Larry's so it wouldn't be too surprising if their fingerprints turned up in his house, but their fingerprints would appear on the top layer of doorknobs and so forth, showing that the men were there very recently. Mine would be even harder to explain. I'd wiped down the medicine bottles, but I might have left prints on doorknobs and other surfaces.

I hurried on so I wouldn't call attention to that problem and worry everyone else. "The police can look at known criminals, notice patterns in neighborhood crime and so forth."

"Wait a minute!" Arnold jumped in his seat. His fork went flying, and he almost knocked over his water glass. He grabbed for it and settled it back into place. "There was another break-in in that neighborhood. I noticed it in the paper, because it was near where Larry lived. No one was home, no one was hurt, but they stole some electronics."

Jen held her pen poised above the paper. "Do you remember when that was?"

"Within the last week, I think."

"I'll track it down." Jen winked at me. She was definitely

auditioning.

Joe passed the fork back to Arnold. "I don't know whether to hope it's a random stranger or not. If it is, we might never learn the truth. Larry won't have closure until he knows for sure that he's innocent."

We all nodded.

"Do I put Larry on the suspect list?" Jen asked.

Several people said no, but I nodded. "We're not trying to change what happened. We're trying to reveal the truth. If it turns out he did kill Pamela, I'm sure it was an accident or something to blame on the drugs. But we need to know."

Clarence put his hands over his face. "I don't think I want to know that."

"We can't control the outcome," I said. "We can only search for clues and hope to find the truth. Back to suspects, any ideas?"

The silence stretched longer. I used the time to get through some kung pao chicken. It was milder than I usually liked, but that was probably best, since I hadn't quite regained the iron stomach I'd had before my injury.

"Someone who wanted to buy Larry's house?" Clarence didn't sound convinced by his own idea. "It can be hard to get in those communities. People sometimes have to wait for a year or more for a home to become available, especially one like Larry's, on the golf course."

Marty wrinkled her nose. "Those houses go for half a million dollars now. Do you really think someone with that kind of money would commit a murder in order to get in there sooner? Wouldn't they simply try to buy their way in? Surely they'd find someone willing to sell, if they offered enough."

"I think the more money you have, the more likely you're willing to commit murder," Joe said. "Plenty of rich people think they can get away with anything."

"What about a real estate agent?" Arnold said. "A sale like that would have a huge commission."

I glanced at Jen. She shrugged but wrote it down. She already had a full page of notes, but I didn't think we'd come up with much. We all knew we were reaching. Plus, Mayor Todd had said developments were springing up faster than they could be filled. That didn't prove no one would kill for a prime spot on a golf course, but I wouldn't put this in my top ten theories.

On the other hand, since we only had about three theories, maybe this one would make it to the top five by default.

"What do we know about Pamela?" Jen asked. "She's younger than Larry, she has two kids, and she's dead. That's all I've heard."

"Good point," I said. "She's the dead one, but we keep thinking in terms of Larry, focusing on how this affects him. What if the killer was someone from Pamela's past, and Larry's presence was incidental?"

"She might have had a boyfriend before she met Larry," Marty said. "We believe she married Larry for his money, but that might not make a difference to a jealous lover. In fact, if she was dating someone whose ego was tied to his, well, virility, having a woman leave him for an older man might feel like a huge insult."

Joe slid his arm over her shoulders and leaned in. "Come on, baby, you know we older men can still satisfy."

She turned to him with a playful smile. "I know it, but younger men might not."

Arnold and Clarence looked at each other and made gagging noises.

In her best stern mother voice, Jen said, "Do I have to separate you two?"

I cleared my throat to get everyone's attention. "Okay, it's worth looking into any ex-boyfriends. But it could also be someone angry at Pamela for a completely different reason. You hear that sex, money, and revenge are the top reasons for crime, but actually it's more complex than that. Poverty, addiction, mental illness, peer pressure, even politics and religion can play roles. We need to look into her daily life, now and before she married Larry. Did she have any arguments with anyone? Any long-running feuds? Any history of drugs or gambling? Maybe she owed someone money."

"Maybe she married Larry because she *needed* money." Arnold gestured with his fork, and a piece of noodle went flying. He didn't seem to notice. "Marry a rich guy, pay off her debts. But he wouldn't loosen the purse strings, so she drugged him, but her bookie or dealer got tired of waiting and came after her."

Jen got up and retrieved the noodle from where it stuck to a cabinet. She tossed it in the sink and rinsed her hands. "Was he a rich guy? The house was valuable, but beyond that?"

"I wouldn't say rich," Clarence said. "When you retire, you need to make sure your investments can support you for the rest of your life, however long that is. Larry should be doing okay, and he has the house if he needs to buy in to a senior living community. But if Pamela had huge debts, Larry couldn't pay them without draining the investments he needed to support himself and her."

"Okay." I rubbed my temples. "We can theorize all we want, but we need some evidence based on things Pamela actually did or said, not just guesses about what someone like her might have done." We now had plenty of options, but I wasn't sure any of our ideas would hold up to scrutiny. We'd have to work through each one. I might be grateful for Jen's notes after all.

"I don't think she had much of a life since she married Larry," Dad said. "From the sound of things, the two of them stayed home most of the time. She saw him and her kids, and that's about it."

"That might make it easier," I said. "People don't usually wait months for revenge. We shouldn't neglect her life before Larry, but we can start with the last month. Even if she rarely left the house, she must have gone shopping once in a while. She might've had run-ins with neighbors."

"How do we do any of this?" Arnold asked. "I have to admit, I was envious when I heard about your investigation of Sunshine Haven, but I didn't realize things got so complicated. Damn it, Jim, I'm a doctor, not a detective!"

"Let's divide up the list," I said. "I'm sure we all have skills we can bring to the work. We need to look into Larry's kids. Does anyone have contact info for them?"

Clarence sat up straighter. "It should be in my files for Larry."

"All right, that's your first task," I said. "Do you suppose the police notified Larry's children that he's in trouble?"

No one could say for sure. He hadn't been arrested, and he wasn't exactly the victim of a crime, at least not one the police were currently investigating.

Clarence sank down again. "I'll tell them. Won't that be fun."

"We should try to meet Pamela's children," I said. "Anyone know their names?"

No one could come up with names for the kids or even remember Pamela's last name before she married Larry. They sure hadn't taken much interest in their friend's new wife.

"How about this?" I said. "Dad and I will go to the hospital in the morning and try to see Larry. If the police have someone stationed in his room, we'll be limited in what we can discuss, but I doubt they have the staffing to bother with that. In any case, we can see how he's doing, if he seems more alert as the drugs leave his system."

"Maybe he'll remember more as his faculties come back," Marty said. "Oh, I hope so."

"Maybe," I said, "but even if he saw something, he won't make a reliable witness. Still, any new information could help us, and we can ask about his kids and Pamela's."

"I'll take notes," Jen said.

"I can handle that," I said.

I wasn't trying to leave her out, but I didn't think we needed the whole group trooping around everywhere, and I could take notes just fine on my own—at least if I could sit down. It was no longer easy taking notes while standing, since I needed the cane for balance if I had to stay on my feet for long. I wanted Dad there so Larry would feel more comfortable, but I didn't want a packed room. No doubt Joe, Clarence, and Arnold wanted to see Larry as well, but as a journalist, I might pick up on something that the others wouldn't.

Fortunately, Marty addressed Jen. "Why don't you and I focus on tracing Pamela's activities recently? People will be more likely to talk to a couple of attractive ladies than these old farts, especially if it turns out she was doing yoga or Zumba or something."

Jen perked up at that suggestion.

"Is there anything I can do?" Arnold sounded plaintive.

I was struggling to come up with jobs for everyone, but I didn't want to exclude anyone. Despite the concern for their friend, and the stress of the situation, the mood in the room was optimistic. I knew from our last investigation that people enjoyed being part of something like this, solving problems, uncovering crimes, fighting for justice. That didn't end because you'd retired from your regular job. If anything, it probably made the change of pace more appealing.

"Talk to your doctor friend," I told Arnold. "Get all the info you can about Larry's condition. See if he'd be willing to testify in court."

He saluted. "On the case, boss."

I leaned over to see Jen's notes. She was on a new page, listing everyone's assignments. She'd certainly latched on tight to this new distraction.

"Arnold talks to the doctor. Clarence looks for contact information on all the children." I looked up at him. "Do you think you can find out about a will?"

"Certainly. I have a copy, unless he changed it after he

married Pamela. He said he would, but I don't think he ever did. He didn't give me a new one."

"Can you find out for sure?" I asked. "We'll ask him tomorrow, but if he did something while drugged, he may not even remember it."

"It depends on whether he filed it. If it's in his house . . ." Clarence shrugged. "I'll see what I can do."

Jen made a note. I checked her list again. I might contact a police detective I knew to see if I could get more information that way, but I could keep that on my personal list.

"Dad and I will go to the hospital. Marty and Jen will trace Pamela's recent activities. Joe . . ."

"I'll canvass the neighbors," he said. "I've met several of them through Larry, so I think they'll talk to me."

"I've met some too," Arnold said. "I'll help as soon as I'm done with the doctor."

"Don't get in the way of the police," I said. "We don't want to trip over each other."

Arnold rubbed his hands together. "Hey, maybe if we talk to people *after* the police, they'll tell us what the police said."

"Worth a shot." I paused to study the remaining food and took another scoop of fried rice. "I guess we have a plan for tomorrow."

I hoped no one would suggest getting started right then. It wasn't that late, but it had been a long day and I was feeling my age. Maybe I was even feeling *their* age, although only Clarence really looked worn out.

"Tomorrow." Arnold hoisted a box of chow mein as if giving a toast.

Dad lifted his glass. "The Coffee Shop Irregulars are on the job."

"The what?" Jen asked.

Dad explained the name.

"It's very good." Arnold giggled. "We should get T-shirts and ballcaps."

"Maybe we should keep a lower profile for now." I lifted my water glass, only half wishing it held whiskey instead. "Here's to proving Larry innocent, finding Pamela's killer, and making the world a better place. To the Coffee Shop Irregulars"

They all raised their glasses. "To the Coffee Shop Irregulars."

It was going to be an interesting week.

Chapter Seven

DAD AND I headed to the hospital in the morning. The clear blue skies and pleasant temperatures, low seventies in early December with hardly a drop of humidity, contrasted with the holiday decorations displayed on homes and businesses. The beautiful day contrasted even more with our errand.

The man at the desk in the lobby gave directions to Larry's room. Upstairs, we headed past the nurses' station and rooms with open doors. We didn't see a policeman on duty in the hallway, but raised voices came from Larry's room.

We stopped at the doorway. Larry sat up in bed, looking weak and frail. Four people stood around the bed, voices raised.

A woman in scrubs strode up beside us. "You here for him too?"

Dad nodded.

"Keep them quiet, or I'll throw them out." She spun away, trotting toward the sound of beeping in another room.

Dad and I stepped into the room. The other people paused in their tirade to study us. On each side of the bed stood one man and one woman. The ones to the right were probably in their late twenties or early thirties, while the ones to our left were closer to my age.

"Isaac!" Larry called out as if begging for a lifeline. He squirmed to sit up straighter.

Dad eased past the pair on the left side of the bed, nudging them back so he could stand at Larry's side. "You're looking better."

The man on the opposite side of the bed threw his hands into the air. "Now what? Who the hell are you?"

Dad stared at him with all the solemn strength of his seventy-six years. "A friend of Larry's, here to look out for his interests."

"I'm Kate Tessler." Before they could ask why I had any business there, I added, "Who are all of you?"

The woman on Dad's side turned to me. She was probably close to fifty, though she might be younger and simply very tired. "I'm Wendy, Larry's daughter. This is my brother, Heath."

Heath scowled, but he gave me a quick nod. He was likely younger than Wendy by three or four years. He wore a white shirt and dark slacks appropriate for an office, but no jacket or tie.

"You're in town?" I asked. I mean, obviously, but they'd both gotten here quickly if they came after news of the murder.

"Yes, we got in yesterday." Wendy stepped closer to me and lowered her voice. "Pamela said she was putting Dad into a home. She asked us to come out and help move him. We wanted to see for ourselves how he was."

The other man, about thirty with shaggy dark hair, tossed his arms up again. "He has dementia! What did you expect at his age? Of course Mom wanted to put him away."

Four voices rose in a babel. I leaned back to glance down the hallway. A woman at the nurses' station looked up from making notes.

I stepped farther into the room and clapped my hands. "All right, enough! You all need to get out of here before you're thrown out. Let's go to the lobby and discuss this."

They grumbled, but they followed me. No one had yet questioned my authority. That might be a sign of my natural leadership. More likely, they were confused and miserable and wanted anyone to take charge.

We came out on a mezzanine that looked over the big, open lobby below. The seating area on the mezzanine had comfortable chairs, and it was far enough away from the patients not to bother them or the nurses. We shouldn't attract much attention there. I waved everyone to the seats. They lined up like they had in the hospital room, two on one side of a coffee table and two across. That left me at the head of the table.

I leaned my cane against the inside of the chair's arm and shrugged out of my shoulder bag. I wouldn't pull out my notebook yet, as many people wouldn't speak freely if they saw me taking notes. Instead, I surreptitiously started a recording app on my cell phone, left it in my shoulder bag, and set the bag on the coffee table between us.

I gave everyone a neutral smile. "All right, we have Heath and Wendy, who are Larry's children. I take it you two are Pamela's children."

The man, slumped in the chair with his arms crossed, merely grunted. The woman said, "That's right, I'm Vanna and that's Vander."

"I'm sorry for your loss," I said.

Vanna pressed her lips together, blinked rapidly, and nodded. She, at least, seem to have some feeling of grief. She had thick brown hair pulled back into a ponytail with strands escaping around her face.

Light brown hair.

"Oh—I'm sorry to ask this, but did you find . . . your mother?" I'd almost said, "the body," but that seemed so impersonal.

Vanna nodded and gulped, her gaze bouncing around the room.

Vander shot his sister a glare. "Hold it together. We have to deal with these creeps." He gestured toward Heath and Wendy.

Heath sat forward. "It's perfectly reasonable for us to ask questions—"

At the same time, Wendy said, "We're sorry about Pamela, we really are, but—"

I held up my hands again. "All right, everyone take it easy. This isn't the time to fight with each other."

It was exactly the time most people would start fighting, when an unexpected death had everyone on edge. I wouldn't be surprised if Pamela's kids were already thinking about her estate, in addition to wanting her murderer caught. Meanwhile, Larry's children clearly intended to protect their father, which as a bonus could mean protecting their own inheritance.

Still, they would hardly make those arguments in front of me, so they settled down for the moment.

"Who are you again?" Vander grumbled.

"Kate Tessler. I'm investigating the situation." Let them interpret that how they would. It was illegal to impersonate a police officer. It was not illegal to let them assume you were with the police.

To ward off any questions about my actual right to investigate, I plowed ahead. I turned to Wendy and Heath first. "I understand you both live some distance away. You came in yesterday?"

They nodded.

"Did you get a chance to see your father before—when was the first time you saw him during this visit?"

"Last night," Wendy said.

"In the damn hospital!" Heath added.

"You didn't try to see him at home yesterday?" I asked.

"We were going to," Wendy said. "We went to the house at five. Dad had been taken to the police station, the police were all over the house, they wanted to talk to us, and by the time we found the police station where he'd been, he was at the hospital."

I wanted to find out whether they had an alibi for the time of Pamela's death, preferably without being too obvious about it. I tried to sound casual. "Unlucky timing. Too bad you couldn't get there a couple of hours earlier."

"We wanted to go right away," Wendy said. "Or at least I did. Pamela said to come at four, but I forgot to change my watch and I missed the time zone difference. By the time I realized my mistake, roused Heath from his nap, and we drove over, it was five."

"Oh, she knew you were coming?"

Wendy nodded. "She knew I was. We didn't tell her Heath was coming too. We weren't sure he'd be able to get away from work. He took a red-eye flight to make it."

I leaned forward to see Heath fully. His clothes didn't look like he'd slept on a plane in them, but the dark circles under his eyes could be from a long night and jet lag.

"So you got in yesterday morning?" I asked.

He nodded. "Seven a.m. Man, I'm tired. I can't sleep on planes. And now all of this."

"What did you do between getting in and going to your father's house?"

"Slept a couple of hours. Not enough. Worked out in the hotel gym. Showered, had lunch or whatever you call it in the middle of the afternoon. Tried to nap again." He rubbed his face. "Tried to feel human again."

"We got together for a couple of hours yesterday afternoon," Wendy said. "We wanted to discuss the situation, make a plan." She lifted her hands. "I guess everything's changed now."

Vander shot out of his seat. "That's right, everything's changed in your favor. You got rid of our mother."

Heath started to push himself up, but then he sank back with a groan. "Oh, shut up. I don't have the energy for this."

"We may not have liked our father marrying your mother," Wendy said. "We may not have cared for her. But that doesn't mean we wanted her to . . . we didn't want this to happen."

Vander kept looming over everyone. Maybe I could knock him back a step.

I turned toward Vander and Vanna. "Why are you two

here?"

"What do you mean?" Vanna asked.

"Here, in the hospital, now."

For a moment they simply stared at me. I thought it was a reasonable question. It didn't sound like either of them had been close to their stepfather, and they sure weren't here to comfort him.

"Van wanted—he said—" Vanna glanced at her brother, away, back again. "We wanted to find out more about what happened. It was *awful*. I'm so—I can't—" She shook her head.

Vander remained standing. "Someone killed our mother. It might have been Larry."

Wendy and Heath started to protest.

I grabbed my cane and shoved myself to my feet so I could glare at Vander from closer to eye level. "That's all the more reason you shouldn't be talking to him. You don't want to interfere with a police investigation. Leave it to the authorities. I think you should go home, start thinking about your mother's funeral or memorial, all the things you have to take care of now she has passed. Did she leave a will?"

Vanna got up. "I don't know. Mom wasn't always big on planning."

"She shouldn't need one," Vander said. "Everything should go to us."

"She was married, so we'll see about that." I held out my arm, gesturing toward the exit. I wanted to get as much information as possible, and maybe having the two sets of kids arguing would help with that, but it wouldn't be good for any of them, or for Larry.

"I'll be back in a minute," I told Wendy and Heath.

I walked with Vander and Vanna, leaving my bag and the recording phone behind. I stopped in the wide hallway near the elevators and turned to them. "I suppose the police had a lot of questions for the two of you. Where you were yesterday afternoon, that kind of thing."

Vander merely grunted.

"I went to Mom's house right after work." Vanna bit her lip. "I was worried because Larry's children were coming that afternoon, but Mom said we didn't need to be there, but I called to make sure, and she didn't answer or call back. We talk every day, and she almost always answers the phone right away. I guess maybe she was already . . . gone."

"What time did you get to her house?"

"It must have been four fifteen or four twenty." Vanna looked at her watch, as if it would remind her. "My shift ends at four—I'm a checkout clerk at the Walmart in Chandler—and it takes about fifteen minutes to get to Mom's house."

Clarence had seen her at around four twenty, so that checked out.

"Do the police have a time of death?" I asked.

"I don't know. I was pretty upset yesterday. I'm not sure they said."

I turned to Vander. "Did you get any idea? If they wanted to know where you were at a specific time, that might be a clue."

"Who cares?" Vander tapped his foot. "Larry did it. Everyone knows that." He turned away but swung back again. "Yeah, I have an alibi for that afternoon, but I don't have to prove it to you. The police know where I was, and they know I have no reason to kill my own mother." He glanced at Vanna and jerked his head toward the elevators. "Let's get out of here."

"Hang on," I said, "where can I reach you if I have more questions?"

"Don't bother." Vander ran his hands through his dark hair, messing it up even more. He was actually fairly good-looking, if you liked the moody, tormented type. "What's the point?"

"The point is finding out who killed your mother. Don't you want to know?"

"I already know." His eyes were shiny. Was his anger really grief?

"Van," his sister murmured. "We don't know for certain it was Larry. I can't believe he would do that. Why would he?"

Vander shrugged. "His mind's gone, and now they're saying he was drugged up too."

"What about the break-in?" Vanna seemed to be studying the pattern in the carpet.

Right, the break-in. "Did the police ask you if anything was missing?"

She nodded without looking up. "Mom's jewelry box. I'm not sure what else."

"What's with all the questions?" Vander asked. "If you're with the police, shouldn't you know all this stuff?"

"I'm not with the local police." That was true enough.

"Whatever." Vander grabbed Vanna's arm. "Come on, let's go."

They got into the elevator. The doors slid closed as I pondered what I'd learned. Vanna had found the body. Could she have *caused* the dead body? Could she have arrived, killed her mother, called the police, and claimed Pamela had been dead when she got there? It depended on how clearly the police could identify the time of death, and how close that was to Vanna's arrival. If Pamela had been killed before four o'clock, for certain, Vanna's alibi should be good. I couldn't imagine a checkout clerk at Walmart could disappear for at least half an hour with no one noticing.

Vander did not make a good first impression, and he was probably the "layabout" Clarence had disliked. Still, it wasn't fair to judge him based on his behavior today, in a time of great stress. Besides, he was right that we hadn't identified a good motive for Pamela's children to kill her. Vander was promoting the idea that Larry had killed Pamela, and Pamela's children should inherit from her. But they still wouldn't inherit from Larry, and he was the one with money.

Maybe they hoped to put Larry away and claim fifty percent of the house. A quarter of a million dollars, even split between the two of them, would be a lot for most people. If that was the plan, they'd gone about it in a roundabout way. If they were willing to kill their own mother, why not kill Larry as well?

I rubbed my temples. I was gathering a lot of information, but I wasn't sure how much of it was relevant or even made sense. Maybe I could turn it all over to Jen and let her prove herself by sorting it.

Unfortunately, Heath and Wendy were more likely suspects. I didn't want to be the one who found evidence against them. Dad and his friends wouldn't be happy if they'd asked me to help Larry and I wound up getting his children convicted of murder.

Still, the truth was the truth. I had to believe that uncovering it would be best in the long run.

Sadly, "best" didn't always mean least painful.

Chapter Eight

I TURNED BACK toward the seating area where Wendy and Heath waited. She'd said they'd been together that afternoon, but could anyone else confirm where they were? If not, they could have committed the crime together. It looked bad that they were both in town when we'd assumed they were far away.

On the other hand, if they'd planned to murder their stepmother, would they have made it so obvious they were in town? Many murders were unplanned, the results of fights or domestic violence, but this one was more complicated. If the murder had been planned, as the possibly fake break-in suggested, I'd be more suspicious of the people who claimed alibis than those who didn't.

I paused at the seating area, studying Larry's children. Wendy stared into space while Heath tapped at his phone. It didn't seem like I'd hear evidence of a crime on my recording.

Vanna had confirmed that Pamela expected Larry's children to come over that afternoon, so that much was probably true. They could have gone early for some reason, maybe planning to reason with Pamela rather than kill her. Maybe they'd fought. Heath and Wendy didn't seem particularly close, but they still might protect each other.

Or if Heath and Wendy had planned and committed the murder together, they might have snuck out of their hotel, killed Pamela, snuck back into the hotel, and then left in a more obvious way, calling attention to themselves and assuming their alibis of each other would protect them.

Oh well. The police would check alibis unless they decided to dismiss the whole thing as a burglary gone wrong. For now, we couldn't cross off any of the four kids from the suspect list.

I returned to my seat. "What are your plans now?"

They looked at each other for a long moment.

"I guess we have to make some," Wendy said. "Everything's changed."

"Did the police tell you to stay in town?" That would be a sign they were considered suspects.

"We haven't talked to anyone who seems to know anything useful," Heath said. "I was planning to fly back to Hong Kong Sunday night."

Wendy frowned. "Everything yesterday was so confusing. I don't think they said we couldn't leave, but I suppose I'll make plans to stay with Dad. He'll need help."

"And you'll get a break from your teenagers." Heath smiled as he said it.

Wendy gave a little shrug and smile in return. "Maybe they'll appreciate me more when I get back."

"It's good you're here," I said. "Had you met Vander and Vanna before?"

"No. We didn't attend the wedding. I feel bad about it now, but Mom hadn't been gone very long, and I couldn't tolerate seeing that woman with Dad. May she rest in peace," Wendy added, clearly as an afterthought.

"I couldn't get away from work," Heath said.

Wendy shot him a look. "You didn't choose to get away from work. You managed to get away this week, when we were worried—" She broke off.

"Yeah, I came this week, and look at what I walked into."

"If you'd paid more attention earlier—"

"Don't give me that. You like to play the attentive daughter, but when's the last time you saw Dad?"

"I was trying to make a point."

"You told him he shouldn't remarry so soon, but you wanted to protect your inheritance."

"I certainly didn't want some tramp as young as me spending it all and leaving Dad broke! Did you?"

"I don't need Dad's money." Heath rubbed his eyes. "I guess I'm glad to be here, or I will be, once I catch up on sleep and things settle down." He gave me a smile that tried a little too hard to be charming. "We weren't Pamela's biggest fans. No reason to pretend otherwise. I still think she was a gold digger. If anyone can prove otherwise, I'll apologize and put flowers on her grave."

"Can we go?" Wendy asked. "I want to get back to Dad. Now that those two are gone, we won't fight, I promise."

"All right," I said. "Your father needs you right now. Focus on that."

Was there any chance that his children had killed Pamela and now planned to get rid of him?

Even if Heath and Wendy had killed Pamela, surely they

wouldn't target Larry yet. It would make more sense to wait until he was out of the hospital, and then arrange an accident, or simply follow Pamela's plan to put him in a home, with his children taking over his finances.

All the same, maybe I'd have a quiet word with the nurses and ask them to keep an eye out.

We all headed back toward Larry's room. I could collect my father and see if he'd learned anything from Larry.

AFTER LUNCH, DAD, Jen, and I gathered in our living room. It was an even more casual "war room" than the kitchen, but I could turn sideways on the couch and put my leg up on pillows. Dad sat on the other end of the couch, and Jen had the easy chair with a lap desk for her notes.

Jen had been gathering the reports from our field team. "Arnold talked to the doctor. He'll testify that he believes Larry was being sedated. He can't give a definite diagnosis about the dementia, one way or another, until Larry is off the drugs."

"He seemed better already this morning," Dad said. "The hospital will release him tomorrow, but he can't go home until the police finish with the crime scene. His children will take him to their hotel."

Jen added to her notes. "Arnold is now with Joe canvassing neighbors. They should make good progress, since a lot of people in that neighborhood are retired and may be home during the day. They haven't run across any police yet."

"Aren't you supposed to be with Marty, tracing Pamela's

activities?" I asked.

"Yeah, about that." Jen gave me a sheepish smile. "We checked social media, but we didn't find any accounts for Pamela. Marty is doing a background check through some online site. We told Joe to ask neighbors if they knew whether Pamela was in any clubs or classes."

"It's a start." I didn't mind that Jen was learning how tricky investigation could be. It was easy to say you'd find out something, but not always easy to do it.

"Anyway, on to Clarence," Jen said. "He got the contact info for Larry's kids, but of course they already knew about the murder."

We'd told Jen about our morning activities, and I gave her the recording to transcribe later. Dad hadn't learned anything else, except that Larry had slept from the time we returned him to his house—as far as he could remember—until he heard Vanna screaming.

"Clarence is now doing some financial and legal investigation," Jen said. "Get this. Larry's son, Heath, filed for guardianship last spring. Clarence found the paperwork in the local probate court."

"What would that mean, guardianship?" I asked.

"He could make legal decisions for Larry. The application claimed Larry is incompetent, but it never got as far as a psychological evaluation."

"Huh." I scratched Harlequin, who had settled against my leg again. "When was this?"

Jen checked her notes. She looked cute with her reading glasses halfway down her nose. "Late May, a week before Larry married Pamela."

"I remember that," Dad said. "Larry was heartbroken that his kids didn't approve, but he still went through with the marriage. In fact, they got married right away in the courthouse. Larry said it didn't matter, since his kids wouldn't come to a wedding anyway, but I got the impression something else was going on. Maybe they wanted to get married quickly as a check against Heath."

Jen looked up over her reading glasses. "Best guess, Heath wanted to prevent Larry from getting married. But going through the guardianship process would take too long, especially with Heath living overseas, so he dropped it after the wedding. Problem is, the application supported Pamela when she claimed Larry had dementia and was incompetent."

Dad shook his head. "Be careful what you ask for."

"Yep. Anyway, Clarence didn't find another will filed for Larry, but he's waiting for a callback from Larry's lawyer. The old will divides his estate unevenly between his children. Wendy gets more, probably because she doesn't seem as well-off as Heath."

"So maybe more of a motive for Wendy, but less for Heath," I said. "Although plenty of people are anxious to get more money, whether they need it or not, especially if they think someone 'less deserving' will get it instead."

"I forgot to ask Larry if he made a new will," Dad said. "Either to give money to his kids, like he told Clarence he would, or one that favored Pamela. I guess it doesn't matter now. He can make another will. I hope he and his children can patch things up."

"That shouldn't be too hard, now that Pamela is out of

the picture," Jen said.

Dad made a face. "Heath is biting his tongue not to say, 'I told you so,' and it's still coming out every third time. Wendy is in full mothering mode. We might have gotten Larry out from under Pamela's thumb only to have his children take over his life."

I nudged Dad with my toe. "Give Larry some credit. And the rest of you. I for one wouldn't stand against the Coffee Shop Irregulars."

"He feels guilty about marrying Pamela. It didn't take him long to learn that she really was out for his money. He might give in to his children simply to make up for not listening to them before." Dad sighed. "And I guess that's his decision, as long as his kids didn't kill Pamela. If they did . . . that might break him."

"Let's fight one battle at a time," I said. "We figure out the truth. If it turns out to be bad for Larry, we stand by him."

"What else?" Jen sifted through her notes. "Oh, the break-ins. I confirmed that there have been two others within about a mile of Larry's house. The papers didn't have much information, but they were daytime break-ins, no one home, and apparently no suspects yet."

"I'd like to know more about those," I said. "Why don't the police think this could be part of the same pattern?"

"Don't you have a police friend?" Dad asked.

"I thought about contacting Detective Padilla, but I decided to hold off. She doesn't appear to be involved with the murder investigation, but if she finds out we were at Larry's house, she'll feel obligated to let the officers in charge know.

I don't want to lie to her or dodge questions, so I'll wait a bit."

I scratched my scar where it itched. "I guess I could call Todd. As mayor, he might know more or be able to find out more."

"Ooh. Looking for an excuse to call hunky Mayor Paradise?" Jen batted her eyelashes. "Or should we say *major paradise?*"

I looked at Dad. "Would you tell your daughter to grow up?"

"Nope. My daughters can stay little girls forever, as far as I'm concerned."

"Fine," I huffed. "I don't suppose it's worth asking for privacy while I call Todd?"

They both shook their heads.

It was too much trouble to get up and leave the room, especially as Jen would probably follow me unless I locked myself in the bathroom. Anyway, it wasn't like I planned a seductive conversation. I only wanted privacy so I wouldn't have to see Jen making faces and hear her whispering suggestive comments.

I called Todd's cell phone. He couldn't always answer, but at least I didn't have to go through a receptionist. After greetings, I asked him about the break-ins.

"I don't know anything more offhand, but I can call the police for an update. I probably should anyway, after yesterday's break-in and murder. Are you involved with that?" He chuckled. "As an investigator, that is. I know you're not involved in the crime. But if you are, don't tell me."

"Yes, to the investigator part. I'll tell you about it sometime. For the moment, if you can get any info on the break-ins, that would be great. For the thing we discussed yesterday, how urgent is it? Can it wait a week or two?"

He made a low hum. "We have a city council meeting in three days. It would help if I had any new ammo—I mean information—by then."

"Noted."

I thought quickly. It would be easier to focus on one problem at a time, but finding Pamela's murder could take days or weeks, if we managed it at all. And while murder might seem more important, if the city council pushed through approval of a new development that forced people to sell their homes and drove up prices on other properties, that could affect many more people in the long run.

In any case, I wasn't sure what more we could do that afternoon while waiting on information about the break-ins and Marty's online search for Pamela's activities. Maybe switching topics would free up my subconscious to make new connections on the murder.

More likely my subconscious would take a nap, but one could always hope.

"Okay, I'm going to start work on your problem this afternoon," I said. "Will you be available if we have questions?"

"I can clear my schedule between two and three thirty, if that helps."

"Do that. And try to get me that information about the break-ins today, please."

"Will do. Let's have dinner soon and catch up on all of this—and maybe save a little time for things that aren't urgent and don't involve illegal activities."

"Sounds good. Bye." I looked up to see Jen grinning at me and realized I had a big smile on my face. Yeah, I wasn't too old to get excited about spending time with an attractive man. So sue me.

I tried to ward off any comments she might make. "I'm going to ask Mackenzie to come over in an hour and help with this other problem." I started texting Mackenzie, my go-to for any and all problems requiring a computer genius. Our best chance of tracking these guys' illegal activities would be online, and probably in places we weren't supposed to access. "Jen, you can stay for that if you don't have anything else you have to do."

The doorbell rang, derailing whatever she might say. She hopped up to answer it.

"Is Isaac Tessler home?" a man's voice asked.

Jen took a step back and looked through the archway at Dad.

"Who is it?" he asked.

A man whose bearing shouted *law enforcement* stepped into the doorway. "Isaac Tessler? We'd like to ask you some questions about your argument with Pamela Hodge at her house yesterday afternoon."

Chapter Nine

TWO MEN ENTERED the foyer. They weren't wearing uniforms, but they had badges clipped at the waist, and one had a gun in a holster. I quickly swung my legs down. It was one thing to stretch out on the sofa while talking with my family, but it left me feeling vulnerable with strangers—especially the police.

The younger one looked at Dad. "Isaac Tessler? We have some questions for you."

"I've been waiting for you," Dad said.

His gaze narrowed. "Is that so?"

"Well, I wasn't holding my breath." Dad seemed perfectly relaxed and cheerful. "I figured it would take you a few days to find out I was there. If I knew you were looking for me already, I would've gone to the police station to make a statement, but I figured you were busy with more urgent matters."

The officer looked nonplussed.

Jen closed the door behind them. "I might invite you in, but you're already in. I guess you'll take a seat if you want one." She brushed past them, picked up the notes she'd left on her chair, shuffled them together, and sat with the notes facedown in her lap.

"Thank you. I'm Detective Olabarria. That's Detective Quarterman."

We introduced ourselves. Olabarria took the empty chair. He was around thirty, with dark hair and eyes and a chiseled jaw, ridiculously good-looking, as if cast in a TV version of a police procedural. In comparison, the older officer, who was still probably a decade younger than me, faded into the background. Quarterman had a choice of sitting between Dad and me or standing. He chose to wander the room, circling behind Dad and me. I didn't worry about him, since Jen still had him in view.

"So you expected us to find you," Olabarria said. "You don't deny that you were at Pamela Hodge's house the afternoon of her murder."

"Certainly I was there," Dad said. "Larry and I have been friends for years. I wanted to check on him, as Pamela has been saying for some time that he's not well. I talked to Pamela—she was alive, obviously—but I didn't get to see Larry. That was at . . ."

He paused and raised his gaze as if thinking, though I was quite certain he remembered the time, as we'd made notes on our visit.

My phone buzzed with a text. It was sitting on the coffee table, so I leaned forward to glance at the message. I heard a faint sound behind me and sensed Quarterman drawing close to the back of the couch. Was he hoping to read over my shoulder? I made sure my body blocked his view of the phone, in case it was one of the Coffee Shop Irregulars with news.

The text was from Jen: *He can cross-examine me anytime,*

followed by a winking emoji.

I held in a snort of laughter. Fortunately, the phone screen went dark after a few seconds. Or maybe it would've been entertaining for Quarterman to read that about his partner.

"It must've been right around eleven fifteen when I arrived," Dad said. "Just out of curiosity, how did you find me so fast? I suppose the military has my fingerprints on file, if they ever bothered to digitize those old records."

"So you admit that your fingerprints are in the house?" Olabarria said.

Dad smiled artlessly at the officer, the picture of innocence. "I just told you, Larry and I have been friends for years, so no doubt my fingerprints are inside the house somewhere. But not from yesterday. I was only at the door yesterday. I did lean on the doorframe though."

Quarterman drifted back into our view and the officers exchanged glances. "As it happens, the Hodges had one of those doorbell cameras," Quarterman said. "It caught your visit. It might have taken us longer to identify you from the picture, but you were at the police station last night."

Uh-oh. That meant the camera had seen me too. Yet they didn't seem to recognize me.

"That's lucky," Dad said cheerfully. "You have a record of everyone who came by yesterday afternoon."

"The only person who went in was you." Olabarria snapped it as if Dad should crumble at proof of his crimes, but the detective had actually given us some useful information—no one else had gone inside the front door that afternoon—assuming the detective wasn't simply misleading us in order to make Dad nervous.

"Then the killer must have been the burglar," Dad said. "We heard about the break-ins."

"Hmm." Olabarria managed to sound doubtful. "We're looking at all the options. Tell us about your argument with Pamela."

Jen jumped in. "You're making an assumption. Those camera doorbells don't have sound. And they only show what's outside the door, so if Pamela didn't step outside, you wouldn't even see her. What makes you think anyone argued?"

Olabarria glared at her. His glare didn't make him any less good-looking. He probably had a lot of women, and a few men, tripping over their own tongues to give him information. It might chafe that he wasn't getting such results here.

"We're basing our reading of the situation on body language." He looked back at Dad. "You pushed your way inside at one point."

"Fascinating," Dad said. "It must be like watching an old silent movie, but without the cue cards for context. I talked with Pamela for a few minutes. Then I started coughing. Allergies. We don't even get winter off in Arizona. She kindly offered to get me a bottle of water. I stepped just inside the doorway while she got that. I can't imagine I was inside more than thirty or forty seconds."

"Forty-three seconds, to be exact," Quarterman said.

"You talk as if my father is a suspect." Jen chuckled. "Surely you have better leads than that."

"We are not at liberty to discuss the case," Olabarria said.

"Doesn't that make it hard to investigate?" Dad said with a straight face.

The detective frowned at him, no doubt debating whether Dad was making fun of him or was simply a harmless and slightly idiotic old man.

Dad turned his head so he could wink at Jen and me without the detectives seeing.

Olabarria aimed his frown at our coffee table. I followed his gaze. My phone sat on the table, some water glasses, a couple of magazines, and my cane.

Did he recognize my cane from the camera? It was a basic type, no dragon head or inlaid shaft. Hard to identify. Had they found marks from my cane going around the house? I was mostly on cement except for a stretch of small gravel along the side yard. That might show slight divots where I'd rested the cane.

It didn't matter. I hadn't done anything wrong, and it might be time to describe our activities yesterday. The police would be checking if anyone in the neighborhood had cameras that showed the street. They'd interview Larry, and he might mention his friends' arrival—and mine—even if his memory was muddled.

Still, I hesitated before introducing a subject that would lead to much lengthier interviews for all of us, taking up our time and the detectives', when we had work to do.

Olabarria shifted his piercing stare to Dad. "That's not the cane you had at the door yesterday."

"No. I had one that has four little rubber feet. It's more stable for outdoor walking." Every word Dad said was true, but his statement was misleading. I suspected he was having fun with all of this.

I stayed quiet. Maybe that was the wrong decision, but if I stayed silent, I could speak at any moment. Once I told them I was at Pamela and Larry's house, I couldn't change my mind.

"You say Pamela Hodge was alive at eleven twenty yesterday," Olabarria said.

Dad nodded. "I suppose you have the exact time I was there. We spoke to Pamela's and Larry's children at the hospital yesterday. They said Vanna found the body about four fifteen. The murderer must have come between those visits."

"Assuming everyone is telling the truth," Olabarria said. "The autopsy will help confirm one way or the other. Did you see anyone else while you were there? Anyone in the house or nearby?"

"Only Pamela in the house. She said Larry was napping. Let's see, did I see anyone outside?" Dad leaned back again, his gaze toward the ceiling.

This would be tricky. He obviously did see me, Arnold, and Joe around the house, and Clarence down the street. Would he admit it?

I felt myself tensing and took a slow breath as I told my muscles to relax. Whatever Dad said would be fine. I'd stay in reporter mode, observing until I needed to speak or act.

"I did see a woman with a walker come out of her house," Dad said. "She went back inside before I got to the door."

"Which house?" Olabarria asked.

"Larry and Pamela's. Oh, you mean which house did the

lady with a walker come out of? I'm not sure. Across the street and down a few. I wouldn't recognize her again. When you get to my age, you see plenty of old folks with walkers."

"Anyone else?"

"It's a pretty quiet neighborhood," Dad said.

Quarterman had drifted to the foyer, which led to the kitchen and stairway.

Jen called out, "If you need the restroom, I can show you where it is."

He hesitated before turning back and leaning against the archway into the living room. "That's all right. Simply admiring your home. All three of you live here?"

"Kate and I do," Dad said. "You might have heard of her. She's a well-known journalist." He said it like a proud father, but the detectives stiffened and exchanged glances. They seemed honest and competent enough, based on this small experience, but Dad had notified them that any tricks or misbehavior might get reported. He was definitely having fun.

Olabarria stood. "We know where to find you if we have more questions. You'll be in town?"

"I rarely travel now, with my wife in a nursing home with Alzheimer's."

Olabarria softened. "I'm sorry to hear that. If you think of anything that might help our investigation, please give me a call." He handed Dad a card.

Jen escorted the men out and closed the door behind them. She returned to the living room, threw herself into the easy chair, and blew out a loud breath. "Whew. I'm sweating."

"That was fun," Dad said. "I know you said don't lie."

"And I noticed you didn't," I said.

"That's what made it fun. I wasn't sure it was time to tell them everything about yesterday. We didn't have a chance to discuss it, and you didn't tell them, so I didn't either."

"Oh, so now I'm the responsible adult who is supposed to set a good example? When did that happen?"

Dad merely beamed at me, his eyes twinkling.

Jen sighed loudly. "Speaking as the most responsible adult in the room even if I am the youngest, I don't think you should lie to the police, not least because you could be charged with obstruction of justice. But it chafes that they are allowed to lie to us and mislead us."

"I noticed you went into protector mode," I said. "I can't imagine Detective Quarterman would have found anything by poking around our kitchen, but I'm glad you called him on it."

"We should protect every right we have when it comes to law enforcement. Many experts would suggest not talking to the police at all without legal representation. In any case, we didn't lie, and while you may not have told them everything you know, I don't think you could be prosecuted for covering up a crime, because what we know doesn't point to the criminal."

"Sounds like you've been researching the question," I said.

"Doing my part." Her smile might have been a little smug.

"I was going through the same debate," I said. "I'm used to dealing with authorities in developing countries, where money or connections can get you in or out of trouble. I probably don't have the highest standards when it comes to respecting law enforcement. But it still feels weird to keep secrets from them."

"After Dad's impression of a feebleminded old man, I can't imagine those detectives will be anxious to interview more elderly men." Jen threw her head back and laughed. "Can you imagine Clarence and Arnold dancing around their questions?"

"The mind boggles," I said.

"Now what?" Jen asked.

"Now we wait for Joe and Arnold to report back on their canvass of the neighborhood, and hope Todd can learn more about the break-ins." I checked my phone. Mackenzie had replied to my text. "Mac will be here by two. In the meantime, what do you know about city politics and real estate development?"

Chapter Ten

DAD HEADED TO Sunshine Haven to visit Mom. When Mackenzie arrived, Jen and I took her to the backyard. We didn't want to miss the rare opportunity to be outside on an Arizona afternoon without melting. I stretched out on a lounge chair so I could take the weight off my bad leg.

Mackenzie, a pretty blonde, was finishing college but already got paid big bucks to help people with computer and IT issues. Mac and I had a deal that I'd train her on various life skills—running a business as a freelancer, investigating people, being badass—and she'd be my computer researcher. We didn't use the term "hacker," but I didn't question how she got her information.

I explained the city council situation briefly. A developer, Zane Dale, was trying to push through new developments that would replace poorer neighborhoods and drive up property prices. He donated money to Eric Konietzko's campaign to get elected to the city council. Konietzko was now supporting Dale's building plans. But were bribes involved? And if so, could we prove it?

"How can we get evidence that someone is taking a bribe?" Mackenzie asked.

"That's the problem. Despite what TV shows might have

you believe, it's not that easy to track financial info. We don't know how often the city council guy meets with the real estate developer, or how careful they are about being overheard or seen passing money. Is the developer getting bundles of cash? Are they doing wire transfers to overseas accounts? We don't know."

Mackenzie tapped her closed laptop. "I might be able to dig into his computer activity, depending on his passwords, but if he has secret accounts and accesses them from one secure device, I might never reach it."

"What about following him or tapping his phone?" Jen said. "That second part probably isn't legal, is it?"

"You can buy apps that do it," Mackenzie said. "Depending on the type of phone, you might need access to the physical device or their account information, and it depends on their security settings, whether they have Bluetooth enabled or use mobile Wi-Fi and so forth. But no, it's not exactly legal."

"They could be using cell phones, office land lines, or computers, or they could be communicating only in person," I said.

Jen stared at me. "So it could take weeks to find anything, and that's if he's not especially careful and we manage to look in the right place at the right time."

I nodded. "Any brilliant ideas?"

Mackenzie opened her laptop and frowned at it, as if it was letting her down by not providing answers. "I'll see if he's on social media. Maybe it will inspire something."

We sat in silence for several minutes. I had a reasonably comfortable lounge chair, a cold drink, and some sunshine. I might have looked like I was about to fall asleep, but sometimes the mind works best when the body is most relaxed.

Jen stared into space. "If this was *Scooby-Doo*, the shady real estate developer would be dressing up as a ghost or monster. We'd set traps, run around a lot, and pull off their mask. It's possible watching cartoons has given me unrealistic expectations."

"Yeah, this would be easier with superpowers," Mackenzie said.

"Maybe we can get them to do something stupid," Jen said.

"What, like snorting cough syrup or learning to yodel?" I asked.

Her look might have made me apologize for being a smart aleck if I'd been about forty years younger.

"I *meant* something relating to these crimes. Like maybe we can make the politician think we already have evidence, so we scare him into meeting with the developer again to discuss the situation. It'll be like we're the ones in masks, pretending to be something we're not in order to spook him into revealing himself."

"Here's something." Mackenzie studied her laptop. "He has his relationship status as 'it's complicated,' but it looks like he's going through a divorce."

"How does that help?" Jen asked. "Are we supposed to track him down and flirt with him and hope we can lure him into revealing something?" She looked surprisingly intrigued by the idea.

"We can't demand access to his financial records, but his wife could," Mackenzie said.

"Oh, right," Jen said. "Any woman trying to get a divorce settlement knows she has a man who wants to screw her over. If he's taking bribes, he's sure not declaring them to the IRS. He probably has a secret account so his wife can't find that money."

They looked at me. I raised my fizzy water in a toast. "You're doing fine. Keep going."

"We could approach the wife," Mackenzie said slowly. "Warn her that her husband might be trying to hide money from her. She's in a perfect position to find out more."

"One problem," Jen said. "If he's taking the money illegally, and she helps uncover it, he'll have to return the money, right? He might even go to jail, or at least lose his position, which could hurt her if she's counting on alimony."

Mackenzie glanced at her computer screen. "I'm betting it's an acrimonious divorce. He's saying some snide things about her and posting pictures of himself with sexy young women. Revenge might motivate her more than money."

"I'd still feel bad if we caused her to lose out," Jen said.

"It's her decision," I said. "See if you can set up a meeting, Mac."

My phone buzzed. "Hey, Todd. What's up?"

"I got that information for you, about why the police don't think Pamela Hodge's murder is related to the break-ins."

"Do tell."

"In the previous break-ins, the thief stole cash, medicines, liquor, and keys. This time, he took some jewelry, and maybe some wine. They can't say for sure about the wine, because no one knows how much was there, but the thief didn't take more than a couple of bottles, if that. The keys were still in a dish by the front door. No medicines seem to be missing, either over-the-counter or prescription."

The prescription medicines weren't there, if the break-in took place while we had Larry at the doctor's office. Did that mean we'd narrowed down the time of the murder, or that this was a different burglar who wasn't interested in drugs?

"Another thing," Todd said. "In the two other break-ins in the neighborhood, the suspect was caught on cameras set up to monitor deliveries, either the homeowner's or one across the street that happened to catch a bit of the scene. It looks like the guy came to the front door in a hat and sunglasses and rang to make sure no one was home. Then he went around the side and broke a window. This time, someone approached the house at about the right time, but it doesn't look like the same person. This person is smaller, wore a different hat, and carried a cane."

Right, because this person was me. Whoops. I could worry about that later. For now, I made a note of the useful information: Pamela was attacked close to the time we returned Larry, and apparently no one else approached the front of the house, making the burglary scenario even less likely.

I cleared my throat. "Okay, thanks for the info." Good thing we were on the phone, so Todd couldn't see my face and I didn't have to hide signs of guilt.

"Do you have anything for me?"

"Don't you want to maintain plausible deniability?" I asked.

"I guess so. Um, you're not doing anything illegal,

right?"

Meet with the wife, warn her about her husband. That was doing her a favor and was, at worst, gossip. Get her to spy on her husband . . . that could lead to her doing something illegal but wouldn't necessarily. Ideally, it would uncover his illegal activities, which was better for our community and society in general.

"No, I don't foresee us doing anything illegal," I said. The wife, maybe, but she wasn't one of us.

I glanced at Mackenzie, who was tapping away on her laptop.

"Computer hacking isn't illegal, right?" I asked Todd. "I mean, if Eric Konietzko can't use secure passwords, it's his own fault."

Todd groaned. "I'm going to assume that's a joke."

"You do that. Bye." I hung up. Todd was such a straight arrow; he was fun to tease.

"So." Jen drew out the word. "You and Todd Paradise." She bobbed her eyebrows up and down.

"Purely business." I winked. "For now."

"We should have you two over for dinner. No, we should all go out for dinner. More romantic. You two could meet for drinks first. And afterward . . ."

"I don't need you to play matchmaker," I said.

She opened her eyes wide. "Don't be silly. I simply want to watch the fireworks and taunt you about them later."

"What if I promise to give you a full report the next day?"

"As long as it has plenty of detail."

"Wow, you two are a lot alike, aren't you?" Mackenzie

said.

Jen and I stared at each other.

"No way!" I said.

"We are not!" she said.

Mackenzie burst out laughing. "You looked exactly alike there!"

I doubted that. I was feeling a bit scrawny after the time in hospital and rehabilitation, while Jen had more curves and glowed with an energy that sometimes made me want to hide under the covers. Jen had longer hair and hers was still brown—with the help of dye, I suspected, though I hadn't asked.

Still, we did have some family resemblance, maybe more in personality than in physicality. We'd grown apart during the years I was away, and Jen had seemed resentful when I returned, but we'd had a breakthrough recently, and I enjoyed our return to a more playful relationship.

That was why I hadn't yet turned down her idea of a partnership. I didn't need or want a business partner, but I didn't want to upset our current balance.

"Anyway," Mackenzie said, "the soon-to-be-former Mrs. Konietzko would like to meet us."

"That was fast," I said.

"Yep. She must have been online when I sent the message." Mackenzie leaned closer to her computer screen. "She says we can come to her business this afternoon. Get this, she owns a cupcake shop."

Jen sat up straighter. "You're kidding. This is the best job ever."

"Yeah, until someone starts shooting." I dragged myself

off of the lounge chair. "Let's go."

As I headed for the house, I heard Mackenzie behind me. "I think she's kidding about the shooting. Mostly."

"It's not a daily occurrence," I said. After all, I'd only been shot at once since I returned to suburban Arizona.

Chapter Eleven

We found Carly's Cupcake Connection in a small strip mall, which managed to look cute with bright signs along the pink stucco above the various shop windows. Jen, Mackenzie, and I entered the shop and paused. While my eyes adjusted to the dimmer light after the brightness of outside, my nose took in the scents of vanilla, spices, chocolate, a touch of caramel, and sweet baking. My mouth watered. My brain said, *YES PLEASE.*

Beside me, Jen sucked in a deep breath through her nose. She might have whimpered.

"Can I help you?" The woman behind the counter was probably in her thirties, with dark, curly hair pulled into a ponytail.

"Are you Carly Konietzko?" Mackenzie asked. "Sorry if I pronounced your last name wrong."

"No problem. It won't be mine much longer. You're the one who messaged me?"

"That's right." Mackenzie introduced Jen and me. Jen gazed into the bakery case with wide eyes.

"We might have to order something before we talk," I said. "Otherwise, I think we've lost my sister."

Carly smiled. "Always happy to have paying customers."

We ordered a Boston cream cupcake, a "Caramel All the Way" cupcake, and a carrot cake cupcake with cream cheese frosting.

The phone rang. Carly passed us plates. "Take a seat. I'll join you in a minute and hear whatever it is you have to say about my almost ex-husband."

We managed to cut each cupcake into three pieces so we could each try them all. They weren't huge, especially for the price, but they packed a punch in sugar and rich flavor.

Carly joined us. We raved about the cupcakes. She listened with a small, self-satisfied smile.

"But you're probably wondering why we contacted you," I said. "We have reason to believe your husband may be taking bribes from a developer, Zane Dale."

She made an "ugh" face. "Zane Dale. The name sounds like a hero in an old Western movie, but he makes my skin crawl."

"You've met him then," I said.

"Oh yeah. He invited us to parties a few times. Lots of alcohol, cigars for the men, women in sexy clothes hired to serve food. Eric called it networking. I called it showing off."

"You're not surprised that your husband might be taking bribes?" Jen asked.

"I wouldn't be surprised by much anymore," Carly said. "I used to like that Eric was ambitious. I dated a guy in college who always had big plans but never actually did anything. It took me two years to figure out he was all talk. I didn't want to be with someone like that."

Her lip curled. "There's always a catch. Eric is ambitious, all right, and there's nothing wrong with that, but he likes to cut corners and get by with schmoozing rather than hard work. Who you know, not what you know, that kind of thing."

"You're obviously not afraid of hard work." Jen gave the cupcake case a longing glance. "Your cupcakes are works of art, both in taste and appearance. You're running your own business, and that can't be easy."

Carly looked around her shop proudly. "Eric was supportive of my 'little business' until he realized I took it seriously and wouldn't drop everything at a moment's notice to wait on him. I won't be surprised if he finds a trophy wife as soon as the ink is dry on our divorce papers. I don't care, as long as I don't have to deal with him anymore."

She met my gaze. "So no, I'm not surprised about him and Zane Dale. But I'm not yet sure why you're telling me."

She wasn't what I'd expected, or at least she was more than I'd expected. I knew better than to go into an interview with preconceptions, but that didn't stop the subconscious from making assumptions. Carly was a smart, savvy businesswoman, with no more illusions about her husband. She was ready to move on with her life and had less anger and bitterness than many in similar positions. I didn't think she'd held on to enough anger to demand revenge, and we wouldn't be able to manipulate her even if we wanted to.

I liked her.

"We're trying to collect evidence of his wrongdoing," I said. "We suspect Zane Dale has been bribing Eric to push through approval of new housing developments. Dale may be ready to support your husband in a run for mayor, so he'll have someone in power who owes him favors. We want to hold them accountable for any crimes they have committed and make sure they don't keep using our town as their personal treasury."

Carly thought about it for a minute. Jen shifted forward and opened her mouth, but I nudged her with my knee to keep quiet. It was best to wait until someone raised an argument, or you didn't know which hurdles you needed to overcome.

"I'd rather be done with Eric," Carly said slowly. "I don't wish him ill. I simply wish him out of my life. But you make a good point. If they get away with this, who knows what they'll do in the future?"

"I realize we're asking a lot of you," I said. "I don't know if it will hurt your finances if we stop Eric, maybe even get him arrested." She could probably figure that out on her own, but none of us would be happy if she lost her shop because she helped us destroy her husband.

"I don't want his money. I can take care of myself." Carly frowned at the empty cupcake wrappers on the table. "I have some ugly cupcakes in the back, ones where I messed up the frosting. I usually cut them up for samples. Let me grab them and maybe a pot of tea. Then you can tell me what you have in mind." She headed into the kitchen.

"Yum, more cupcakes," Jen said.

Mackenzie leaned forward and whispered, "As long as she's not actually calling the police right now to report us for, I don't know, collusion or something."

We listened for a minute. Faint sounds came from the kitchen, the clanking of dishes, not a voice on the phone.

Carly returned with a plate of cupcake pieces. Some of

the selections looked different than the ones we'd already tried. I didn't need any more sweets.

I'm not saying I didn't *take* any more.

"All right, assuming I'm willing to help, I'm not sure what I can do," Carly said. "I don't live with Eric anymore, you know."

"You still have ways of getting information about him, right?" Jen asked. "I assume you have a lawyer handling the divorce. Maybe they could demand financial information."

"Blech. Can't we keep the lawyers out of it? They take forever to do anything. Anyway, if Eric wants to keep money from me, he won't make it that easy to find."

"What would he do?" Mackenzie paused with a piece of coconut-topped cupcake an inch from her mouth. "Would he be likely to demand cash and put it in a safe-deposit box or hide it in his house? Would he leave an electronic trail to an account somewhere?"

"He does almost everything on his phone, including banking. He doesn't carry cash at all. But he uses fingerprint access on his phone."

"We can get around that," Mackenzie said. "Do you have something with his fingerprints on it? Smooth glass would be best."

Jen stared at her. "Don't tell me that thing they do in the movies where you put a piece of tape over someone's fingerprints to lift them actually works."

"It's more complicated than that, but if we can get a good copy of the print, I can use the 3D printer at the makerspace to print a slightly raised copy on a fingerprint sleeve."

"Have you done this before?" Jen asked.

"No, I looked it up on the drive over." Mackenzie studied the dwindling cupcake pieces and plucked out one that seemed to be mostly chocolate.

Carly raised an eyebrow. "You three have interesting skill sets. You'll notice I haven't asked whether you have the authority to do all of this."

"Near as I can tell, it's not actually illegal to copy someone's fingerprints." Mac opened her eyes wide in innocence. "What someone does with the copy afterward might or might not be another matter."

"Good to know." Carly had yet to take any cupcake bits. Maybe she got used to the smell, and it didn't affect her as much. Or maybe she immediately scarfed down two or three of each item when they came from the oven, like I would.

"Say I find something that has his prints on it. Then what?" she asked.

"After Mackenzie does her wizardry, we'll need to get his phone for a few minutes," I said. "Does he usually keep his phone on him? Would he put it on the table at a restaurant or leave it in his car or something?"

"It's almost always in his jacket pocket."

I frowned. "Too bad it's December. In hotter weather, you could meet him at an outdoor café, and if he took his jacket off and hung it over the chair, we might be able to sit behind him and reach it. As far as I know, our skill sets do not include the pickpocketing technique to get a phone out of a coat while he's wearing it."

I shot Jen a look. "You can work on that for future cases."

For a second she looked surprised. Then she shrugged and nodded. I might be unleashing a monster.

"What if he came to your place?" I asked Carly.

"He wouldn't take off his jacket. He thinks it makes him look more authoritative."

"His office?"

"I haven't been there in months, but if I came in, I guarantee he'd put his jacket on if he wasn't wearing it already, and he'd stay on the other side of the desk from me. He likes to pretend he can be intimidating."

"What if one of us sets up an appointment with him?" Jen asked.

"Jacket on, phone handy. I doubt you could get it away from him if he's conscious."

"Ooh!" Jen actually raised her hand. "What about someplace like the pool, where he'd have to take off his jacket and put it in a locker?"

Carly wrinkled her nose. "I can't see inviting him to the pool. Plus, then we'd have to get into the men's locker room. You may be onto something though. He's competitive. If I could challenge him to the right thing, or get him to challenge me . . ."

"I have it!" Jen said. "The climbing gym."

We all looked at her with varying degrees of confusion or skepticism.

She nodded. "The kids had a birthday party there a couple of months ago. They have these wooden cubbies where you leave your stuff, so not lockers with locks, and everything's together along one wall, so we don't have to worry about getting into a men's dressing room." She turned to me. "I was thinking you and I could try climbing sometime."

Sure, one-legged climbing might be fun.

"I've never done anything like that before," Carly said.

"They have beginner classes," Jen said. "We can all sign up for a class. Tell Eric you need to see him for some reason, like you need a signature, and ask him to come by there. Then we have to get him to join the class, so he has to take off his jacket and put his stuff in a cubby."

"Lots of moving parts to this plan," Mac said.

Carly's smile slowly grew. "I'll needle him about how he used to be such an athlete and isn't anymore. I'll imply he couldn't get up the easiest wall. Ha! Can't get up, can't get it up. What man could let an insult like that pass? Oh yeah, this could work."

"Really?" Jen beamed.

"He has a mild fear of heights," Carly said. "Not enough to scare him off but enough that he'll think he has to prove himself."

It was ridiculously complicated, but I didn't have a better plan, so I said, "Jen and I can help make sure he's distracted, while Mac gets his phone, does her thing, and returns it. How long do you think you'll need, Mac?"

"Only a few minutes," Mackenzie said. "I'll install a hidden app that lets me get onto his phone remotely."

"This can't possibly all be legal," Carly said.

"Let's focus on the greater good," I said.

"I wasn't complaining," Carly said. "I am so sick of guys like Eric and Zane Dale getting away with the crap they pull. They don't play by the rules, so why should we?"

From the kitchen, a kettle wailed.

"I'll grab the tea," Carly said. "Then we can get down to details. This is going to be fun."

One way or another, at least it should be entertaining.

Jen pulled the plate closer and picked up cupcake crumbs on her fingertip. "Best. Job. Ever."

Chapter Twelve

WE MADE PLANS for the next day. Mac went with Carly to find something that might have Eric's fingerprints. Jen and I turned our attention back to Larry and Pamela. We needed to find out if Joe and Arnold had learned anything in their canvass of the neighborhood, and if Marty had turned up any of Pamela's activities. Rather than cram into our kitchen again, Jen made a reservation at a restaurant with a private back room.

We had time for a quick visit to Mom at the care home before meeting for dinner. The place had become so familiar in the last few weeks. We walked through the lobby and greeted the receptionist. I glanced at the door to the office behind the front desk. My friend Heather Garcia was the director, but I didn't have time to visit with her as well.

Jen and I checked Mom's room, and when we didn't find her there, we tried the solarium. I was getting better at spotting Mom among all of the elderly people in the room, but I still trailed behind Jen. Mom recognized us both and even got our names right, which made this one of her good days.

She told us about the crafts they'd done that morning. At least, they'd done the crafts at some point. You couldn't trust

Mom's sense of time anymore, but she remembered the event and enjoyed it.

"What have you girls been up to?" she asked.

Jen looked at me and raised her eyebrows, asking how much we should share.

I hesitated. It was hard to guess when Mom would remember people. But never mentioning people wouldn't help her memory, and she always did enjoy some good gossip. Besides, she might have insight that could help us.

"Do you know Dad's friend Larry Hodge?"

Mom's forehead wrinkled as she thought. "Yes, Larry and Betty."

If Betty had died in the spring, before Mom's Alzheimer's got bad, Mom must've heard about her death, but she might have forgotten. Had Mom and Betty been close? Would she grieve again when she heard?

"Were you friends with Betty?" I asked.

"Not really." Mom leaned forward and lowered her voice. "She doesn't talk about anything but quilting. That's fine for her, but boring for those of us who don't quilt. I knit, but I don't have to talk about it all the time."

"Well, Larry married a woman named Pamela a few months ago," I said, skimming over the issue of what had happened to Betty. "She's quite a bit younger than Larry, a few years older than Jen and I are."

Mom sat back, her eyes large behind her glasses. "But his children are your age."

"Yes, I don't think they were very happy about the marriage."

I shouldn't have started this. It was too complicated to

explain. But even in her present state, Mom sometimes had good advice, if she understood enough of the situation. I'd often gotten impatient with her advice over the years—it seemed she had an opinion to share on everything—but Mom giving advice was part of Mom being Mom.

"Dad and his coffee group asked us to help out," I said, "because they were afraid Pamela was taking advantage of Larry. Turns out they were right. She'd been giving him drugs to sedate him and keep him quiet."

"Hi, Kate!" a voice called. Zinnia bounced over. She was a teenage volunteer at the home, a plump and pretty blonde who always seemed cheerful. She was great with the Alzheimer's patients and had literally saved my mother's life.

Jen and I greeted her, but Mom was still pondering Larry.

"His daughter gave him drugs?" Mom asked.

Jen took Mom's hand and spoke slowly. "No, Larry married Pamela, who was as young as his daughter. His new wife, Pamela, sedated him. Pamela married him for his money and wanted to incapacitate him."

"That's terrible!" Mom said. "He should have stayed married to Betty. She was boring—didn't talk about anything but quilting—but she didn't do drugs."

I had a feeling I wasn't going to get any useful ideas from Mom after all. At least I hadn't tried to explain about the mayor, the politician, and the developer. That sounded like the start to a joke, but I could imagine spending hours trying to unravel the details.

"Who are you talking about?" Zinnia asked.

"A friend of our father's," I said. "He remarried this year, but it turns out his new wife just wanted his money."

"Huh. I'm glad Grandpa is dating Ms. Garcia instead of someone like that."

"Oh, did they finally . . ." I trailed off.

Heather's relationship with Henry Wilson, Zinnia's grandfather, had been a secret, although not as well-kept as they'd hoped. Zinnia might've found out even if Heather and Henry hadn't yet gone public.

"Um, you know about them?" I asked.

"Grandpa told everyone two weeks ago. It was *dramatic*." She rolled her eyes. "Mom and Dad *aren't* happy, and the aunts and uncles—*they* said Heather is too young for him and probably only after his money, but I don't think that's true. Most of them haven't even met Ms. Garcia, but I have, and I've seen them together. They're happy. Grandma moved to Florida *years ago*, so why shouldn't Grandpa be happy with someone new?"

Maybe to a teenager, anything over thirty was ancient, so a few decades didn't matter. But she was right, a big age gap didn't always indicate a problem. Heather, the director of Sunshine Haven, had met Henry Wilson because he was on the care center's board. They'd bonded when the prior director tried to blame Heather for problems he'd created, and Henry was the one person who listened to her side of the story and found out the truth. I liked both of them, and they seemed to do well together. People of any age could be good or bad, and people could enter relationships for all kinds of reasons. In Larry's case, Pamela as an individual was the problem, not merely the fact he'd married a younger woman. I appreciated the reminder.

We all chatted for a few more minutes, until the attendants started ushering residents to their rooms so they could serve dinner. It wasn't even five o'clock yet.

I said goodbye to Zinnia, and Jen and I walked Mom to her room.

Mom hugged me goodbye. "Love you, baby girl."

She felt both fragile and strong in my embrace. Her scent was subtle, something I didn't notice unless I was very close and paying attention.

Had I thought the goal in coming here was to see if Mom had any insight into our investigation? On some days, she might, but that wasn't her value. Maybe I had subconsciously wanted her to have something useful to say, to prove she could still be useful to society. But if she never did or said anything useful for the rest of her life, she was still our mother, and we loved her. That was enough. She was useful to us, and I suppose as long as she still found some enjoyment in life, she was useful to herself.

Jen drove to the restaurant. When we arrived, she sped up the walk while I was still maneuvering my cane and legs out the door. In the foyer, she paused to talk to the host for about three seconds before swinging left and charging through a section of the restaurant to the back.

My leg ached from too much time sitting. I lurched up to the host.

"I'm with her." I nodded toward Jen.

The androgynous young person looked at my cane and back up at me. "Do you need help? Can I . . ." They trailed off, clearly trying to be accommodating but at a loss. What were they going to do, offer to carry me? Fetch a wheelchair?

Get a burly busboy to toss me over his shoulder?

"I'm fine." I strode—well, hobbled—past them. After a couple of steps, I made myself slow down. Hurrying to prove I was capable would backfire if I stumbled or crashed into a table. Maybe someday I would stop trying to prove I wasn't disabled, when I totally was disabled, and there was nothing wrong with that. Today was not that day.

I concentrated on walking at a leisurely pace. That gave me time to glance around at the decor.

Wow. It was a Mexican restaurant that specialized in seafood, which was odd enough in the desert miles from any sea. Apparently, they decided to lean into the weirdness. The walls were jam-packed with everything and anything related to Mexico, the beach, or the ocean. Thick ropes attached to buoys draped under straw hats and neon beer signs with words in Spanish. A string of chili pepper lights surrounded the door to the back room where Jen had disappeared.

I reached that doorway without mishap, but I hesitated before going in. Something felt off, and it wasn't my stride.

I'd had plenty of experience observing my surroundings and watching for the subtlest signs of danger. I might be out of practice after the last couple of months, and I certainly hadn't expected to feel danger here, beyond the possibility of a tequila hangover or indigestion from spicy food. Still, my senses said something was wrong.

I turned to survey the room. Fortunately, I didn't get the feeling I should hit the deck to dodge gunfire. The young host was still watching with concern. If I dropped to the ground, no doubt they'd call an ambulance.

I scanned the room, forcing myself to ignore the blaring

visual noise of all the decor. The tables had wine bottles wrapped in straw with a candle stuck in the neck. Wasn't that pseudo-Italian rather than pseudo-Mexican?

Wait, I was ignoring that kind of thing.

I'd passed between tables on either side to get through the room. Most of the tables were full. A family with children. Two men in business suits drinking Corona with lime. An older couple. Four young women with enormous margarita glasses, starting their evening with a bang. Another family.

At the closest table to my left, a single person sat facing me—facing the doorway to the back room. He held a large menu, blocking my view of his face, but the hands suggested an adult man.

I took a step forward to see him better. A ball cap came into view. Then a pair of sunglasses.

A lone man wearing sunglasses inside. That's what had triggered my warning sensors. But should I be concerned? The man might be trying to keep a low profile because he was meeting someone for an affair. He might think sunglasses inside made him look cooler. He might simply have forgotten he was wearing the sunglasses and be wondering why it was so hard to read the menu.

The menu appeared extensive, but he'd been studying it for quite a long time without turning a page. The way he held it, up between us rather than at an angle resting on the table, didn't seem natural.

I took another step. If he wanted to keep hiding his face, he'd have to wear the menu like a hat.

He lowered the menu as his wide shoulders heaved with

a sigh. Detective Quarterman glared at me. Yes, I could feel the glare through the sunglasses.

"Good evening," I said.

He gave a brief nod.

"Enjoy your dinner." I turned and stepped into the back room.

Chapter Thirteen

DAD HAD ARRIVED, as well as Joe and Marty. I rounded the table to find a seat where I could keep an eye on the doorway.

The detective's presence could be a coincidence. He might have been hiding because he was off duty and didn't want to make small talk or didn't want the awkwardness of acknowledging someone he barely knew.

But Phoenix was a big place. That made this a big coincidence. Too big.

It was funny imagining Quarterman trying to figure out what Jen and I had been doing at a cupcake shop for over an hour, but I didn't actually want the police to waste their time. In any case, he'd arrived before Jen and I had, since he was seated and had a drink.

So who was he following? Did they seriously consider Dad a murder suspect? Did they think he knew more than he'd shared, which was of course true? Or had Quarterman been following Joe? Maybe he'd spotted Joe and Arnold as they worked the neighborhood and decided that was suspicious.

Oh well. He might overhear some of our conversation from outside the private room, but that merely meant we couldn't confess to any crimes (which was fine, since we hadn't committed any, or barely any) or plan any new crimes (which I hoped we wouldn't be doing anyway).

"FYI, one of the police detectives is right outside." I kept my voice low enough that I didn't think Quarterman would hear, but if he did, so what?

A waitress came in with a pitcher of water and started to fill glasses. Half a minute later, Arnold stepped through the doorway, followed by Clarence. They both turned right, just as the waitress finished filling the last glass and turned to go. The men were blocking her way.

Arnold spun to go the other direction. Clarence, who must not have noticed the waitress yet, almost crashed into him.

Arnold grabbed one of Clarence's hands and put his other hand at Clarence's waist. "Shall we dance?" He turned Clarence in a waltz that was surprisingly smooth given the narrow aisle.

Clarence laughed. "Hey, who said you got to lead?"

The waitress slipped past them out the doorway.

Arnold drew back a step and bowed over Clarence's hand. "Thank you, that was divine. Although I suppose given our surroundings, we should be doing the *salsa*."

"As long as it's not the hokey pokey," Clarence said. "I used to be addicted to it. Then I turned myself around."

Arnold straightened with a groan. "That's such an old joke."

"I like old jokes." Clarence slapped his arm around Arnold's shoulder. "Why do you think I'm friends with you?"

"You're in a good mood today," Jen said as the two men

pulled out chairs and sat.

"You betcha!" Clarence said. "Larry is getting better already. After one day, his mind is clearer, and he's more alert."

"Maybe I should feel bad that woman died," Arnold said. "But I can't, not if she was drugging Larry to keep him quiet so she could put him in a home. For that, I could have killed her myself!"

His voice had risen on the last sentence. We hadn't had a chance to warn Arnold and Clarence about our spy. The rest of us glanced toward the doorway.

Dad whispered something to Clarence, who turned and whispered to Arnold.

Arnold looked over his shoulder and spoke clearly. "Speaking theoretically, of course. I did not actually kill anyone."

"It's funny though," Jen said.

"You talking about me again?" Arnold asked.

Jen shook her head. "Not humorous, but weird. We think Pamela was drugging Larry so she could claim he had dementia and put him in a home. That might work to get him *into* a home, if she didn't have to get him past a doctor who would recognize what was really happening. Then what? The drugs would wear off and he'd go back to normal."

"Maybe she planned to visit him every day," Marty said. "She could give him more of those sedatives. She wouldn't be able to leave town for a long trip or anything, but besides one short visit a day, she'd have her time for herself. No old man to take care of."

"Hey!" Joe said.

Marty leaned into him. "Her loss, of course." She kissed her husband's cheek.

Clarence picked up a napkin, flicked it out, and laid it in his lap. "If she had him legally declared incompetent, it might be hard to get that reversed. She could draw out a legal battle for months, maybe even years. Maybe until he started having real problems or died. The law moves slowly."

"Still, it's not a great plan," Jen said. "It seems like the chances of getting caught are high."

"People often overestimate their own intelligence," I said.

"Was it that much of a risk?" Dad asked. "She could claim she'd meant well and made a mistake. The worst that would happen is Larry would get out at some point, but by then Pamela could have spent all his money or moved it to other accounts. He'd have to prove she'd intentionally lied about him in the first place to take any legal action against her."

"You see why I don't care she's dead?" Arnold said.

We all looked toward the door again.

Arnold lifted his hands. "I'm just saying what everyone thinks. Honesty is the best policy."

"You keep talking like that when there's a detective around, and the only policy you'll need is a life insurance policy," Clarence muttered.

"So Clarence," I said, "did you find out if Larry had a more recent will?"

"His lawyer intimated that he did have a will made in the last year, but of course he couldn't tell me what was in it. I visited Larry this afternoon and he confirmed making a will in Pamela's favor, but he's still pretty tired and struggling to remember details. I figured it didn't matter now."

"I suppose not," I said. "It's more evidence against Pamela, but that's not what we need."

The waitress came back to take our orders, so we paused to quickly scan the menus. I was tempted by the steak and bacon tacos, but I settled for fish tacos with coleslaw and avocado. A somewhat healthy dinner would counteract the number of cupcakes I'd eaten that day, right?

I scooped some salsa onto a chip. "While we wait for our food, why don't you tell us what you learned from the neighbors?" I glanced at Joe. "Unless you think that's a bad idea in the current circumstances." I jerked my head toward the doorway and Quarterman outside.

"I'm afraid we don't have anything worth hiding," he said. "Pamela had only lived there a few months. A couple of the neighbors greeted her when they first moved in, went over with cookies or such. They said she was polite enough, but after that, she didn't do more than wave in passing. They didn't notice anyone visiting her except her kids."

"I looked into her past activities under her maiden name," Marty said. "No criminal record. She's been divorced three times, the last one seven years ago, so it doesn't seem likely an ex-husband came after her now. I'm trying to track them down anyway. We have her work history, but she doesn't appear to have hobbies. No gym memberships, no clubs or classes that we could find. She didn't have any social media accounts, unless they're under a fake name. It's hard to track friends without those links."

Jen had her notebook out. She paused with her pen poised. "No social media seems suspicious."

"Not particularly," I said. "It's true that eighty percent of American adults use social media, but in her age range the percentage would be lower. That leaves twenty to thirty percent who either don't have access, don't want to give up privacy, or simply don't bother. They're not necessarily hiding anything sinister."

Marty nodded. "Plenty of people spend their free time watching TV or have hobbies like knitting that don't take them out of the house unless they join a crafting circle. Maybe she was just an introvert, or didn't like people, or people didn't like her."

"The first time I met her, I wanted to buy her a present," Arnold said. "A toaster for her bathtub."

"What about dating apps?" Jen asked. "Did you check those? Do we know how she met Larry?"

The men exchanged glances and shrugs. "Come to think of it," Dad said, "when I asked Larry how they'd met, he dodged the question. I forgot about that."

"I didn't think of dating apps," Marty said. "Aren't there a bunch of them? And she wouldn't have an active account now. At least, I hope not."

"It's worth checking," Jen said. "You might have to join the apps to see anything though. If she had a dating profile, it could talk about hobbies. Even if she marked herself as no longer looking, maybe she didn't delete the profile. I don't think you'd be able to see her past matches unless you can get into her account, so it won't help find ex-boyfriends."

"I'll see what I can do," Marty said. "I might need to recruit Simon." Simon was her grandson who had taken over the computer store Marty opened decades ago.

"Yes, make him get an account," Joe said. "No dating apps for you."

Marty fluttered her eyelashes. "Are you afraid I'd pick up new men?"

"I know you'd have hordes after you. You might become one of those cougars."

"As if I'd want to deal with more than one man. You're trouble enough."

"I try."

I leaned closer to Jen and whispered, "Should I be concerned about your knowledge of dating apps?"

"I like to read advice columns," she whispered back. "It's a guilty pleasure."

I doubted pursuing Pamela's friends and hobbies would lead to much, since it didn't seem she'd been in touch with many people lately, but you never knew. Maybe she'd hooked up with someone before Larry, and that guy came after her. Maybe we'd turn up someone who knew she had a gambling debt or a history with drugs. Her past could have followed her to Desert Drive.

Still, it seemed like a long way around to get where we wanted to go. It appeared that Pamela had very few current connections: only her children and Larry. Larry might have more info for us once he fully recovered from weeks of being sedated. Her children could be an even better source, given that they'd known their mother for their entire lives and presumably—hopefully—hadn't been sedated for most of them.

I tried to replay our hospital conversation in my mind. Vander thought Larry had killed his mother. Vanna was willing to entertain the idea of a random burglar. Neither of them had suggested Pamela had enemies, but we hadn't directly asked.

"We need to talk to her kids again," I said. "It seems like she was closer to them than anyone else. Hopefully they'll know if their mother was in trouble or if anyone threatened to hurt her."

"You think parents tell their children everything they're doing?" Dad asked. "I mean *I* do of course, but I'm hardly average." He winked.

"You're way better," I said.

"Even if the kids know something, they might not want to tell us anything that would reflect badly on their mother," Marty said.

"If it could catch her killer, they might."

Of course, the waitress chose that moment to enter with a platter of food. If she caught my statement, she chose to ignore it.

Once she left, Dad said, "Back to Pamela's kids. I'm taking Larry to the funeral home tomorrow to start making plans for Pamela's memorial."

Arnold snorted. "Let's set off fireworks and play 'Ding-Dong! The Witch Is Dead.'"

"We might stick with something slightly more tasteful," Dad said. "In any case, I think her children would want to be there to offer their opinions. I'll suggest it."

"Will Larry want them there?" Marty asked.

"If they get too demanding, we can ask if they're going to pay for the funeral," Dad said. "I bet that makes them disappear. We don't have to make any final decisions anyway. The police haven't even released Pamela's body yet. It's more to help Larry start processing the loss."

"Losing her was like losing a year of Mondays," Arnold said.

Marty pointed her taco at him. "He still loved her, or thought he did once. That's the loss he needs to process."

"Maybe you should come with me, Kate," Dad said. "You'll know the questions to ask her children."

"Sure." No pressure there.

By the time we finished eating, I was ready for bed and glad to get a ride home with Dad. Detective Quarterman was no longer at his table, but it hadn't yet been cleaned. Had he darted out when he heard us getting ready to leave? In his place, I wouldn't want to either greet or ignore people I'd interviewed in a murder case as they passed by me.

Or had he raced for his car in order to follow one of our group?

It didn't matter. He wouldn't find anything interesting.

I glanced at Arnold. He was holding on to Clarence's arm but still weaving slightly and giggling as they walked toward the door. He'd had a margarita. Either that was strong enough to get him tipsy, or he was still celebrating Pamela's death.

Arnold's delight at Pamela's death might be suspicious, in the detective's eyes, but it didn't mean Arnold was involved. And Arnold couldn't celebrate by doing anything outrageous, such as desecrating Pamela's grave, because she hadn't been buried yet. So, no problem. Quarterman wouldn't find anything interesting if he followed one of us. He'd waste his time while the real murderer went loose, but we couldn't stop him from doing that.

Meanwhile, I now had a funeral home visit and Pamela's excitable children in the morning, and the climbing gym escapade to entrap a shady politician in the afternoon.

I'd gotten emails from some of my journalism colleagues, expressing condolences for my injury and hopes that I wasn't getting too bored stuck at home while I recovered.

If only they knew.

Chapter Fourteen

DAD AND I picked up Larry at the hospital the next morning. They'd run all the tests they needed and were willing to discharge him, but they didn't want him on his own for a few more days. We'd take him to the funeral home and then to the hotel where his kids were staying. The police had released the crime scene, but the house hadn't been cleaned.

Larry took my hand and held it. "Hello, Kate. I've heard so much about you from your father. I feel like we've met before."

We had, when I'd helped get him out of his house for the doctor's appointment and back in afterward. If he didn't recall that, I saw no reason to remind him.

"I'm glad you're feeling better," I said. "My condolences on the loss of your wife."

"I can hardly believe it." He turned and shuffled toward the doors. "That she's gone. That she was drugging me. The last few months are such a blur. I'm glad that's over, but Pamela . . . she didn't deserve to die like that."

Arnold would disagree, but I nodded. "Whoever did it will be held accountable."

Larry paused right outside the hospital and glanced

around. He spoke softly. "The police think I did it. I can't even say they're wrong. I simply don't remember."

Dad put a hand on his shoulder. "We believe they're wrong. It's not the kind of thing you'd do, and you were in no state to fight anyone."

"I hope you're right," Larry said. "But it wouldn't be the first time I've killed someone." He glanced at me. "In wartime, you understand, and from a distance. Still, that haunts me. I killed because my country told me to. How do I know I wouldn't kill Pamela, maybe by accident in my confusion? The police say it wouldn't have taken strength. Someone hit her in the face, and she fell and hit her head. The fall is what killed her."

That was useful information. Pamela's death might have been an accident. That could lend weight to the idea of a home break-in. If a burglar had reason to think the house was empty, and they found someone inside, they might have hit her and fled. It wouldn't have to be someone specifically trying to kill Pamela.

But why would a burglar assume the house was empty? Did they not realize it was a fifty-plus community with lots of retirees? The doorbell camera hadn't shown anyone coming to the front door besides Dad and me, unless the police were withholding info—entirely possible, but if they had that lead, why were they bothering with the rest of us?

While I pondered this, Dad comforted Larry. Finally, he said, "Whatever happened, we'll find out the truth, and we'll deal with it. Even if the worst is true, I doubt you'd go to jail for hitting Pamela and accidentally killing her, given what she'd been doing and your state at the time."

"Jail is the least of my worries," Larry said. "I'm worried about my soul."

On that note, we got to the car and headed for the funeral home. I hoped Larry wouldn't try to ease his guilt by spending ridiculous amounts of money on a funeral for the wife who'd abused him.

We stepped through the funeral home doors. Arnold and Clarence greeted Larry enthusiastically.

I forced a smile. What fun. Having his friends around him might make this easier on Larry—but only if Arnold kept his opinions to himself.

A young man introduced himself as the funeral home director. His somber words contrasted with his round face and rosy cheeks. "Goodness, this is quite a large group," he said.

"Pamela's children aren't even here yet," Dad murmured.

"Should we wait?" Larry pushed a strand of hair off his forehead. "It's all so much to handle."

"How about I wait out here for them," I said. "Arnold and Clarence can stay with me. When Vanna and Vander arrive, we'll let you know."

Larry, Dad, and the funeral home director headed into an office and closed the door.

Clarence looked around the lobby and shuddered. "Place gives me the creeps."

"You didn't have to come," I said. "I'm sure Larry appreciates your support, but when Vanna and Vander get here, please keep your opinions about their mother to yourself." I gave Arnold a stern look.

He made a motion of zipping his lips and ruined it by

immediately speaking. "I won't start anything. That's all I can promise."

I tried to count to ten but only got to four. Finding patience with these guys was about as easy as being patient with software updates over a slow internet connection when on deadline.

"I hope you had a quiet evening after the restaurant," I said.

The two men exchanged an amused look. "It was lovely," Clarence said.

My face heated. I didn't mean to pry into their personal lives.

"Don't forget that Detective Quarterman may be keeping an eye on some or all of us," I said.

"Oh, that." Clarence shoved his hands in his pockets and turned away. "We have nothing to hide. Not anymore."

Before I could decide if that was a statement that needed pursuing, the door swung open, bringing in a cool breeze, a flutter of dead leaves, and Pamela's children.

Vander looked at me, and his eyebrows rose. "You again?"

"My father is with Larry and the funeral director."

"They started without us?" Vanna's gaze darted around the room and landed on the office door.

"The funeral home needs a lot of information," Clarence said. "They're probably still filling out paperwork. I'm sure you have plenty of time to share your opinions about the funeral or cremation."

She clutched her hands together. "It's just, we don't think Larry should be making these decisions, not while he's still, well, under suspicion."

Vander shoved open the office door.

It hit one of the chairs inside and bounced back, smacking into Vander's hand and knocking him back a step. He growled and pushed open the door again.

I got close enough to see Vander, Dad, and Larry. The funeral home director was mostly out of sight on the other side of his desk.

"You can stop all this," Vander said. "Don't waste the money."

Larry pushed back his chair and got up slowly. "I can afford to give your mother a nice memorial."

Vander crossed his arms and leaned against the doorframe. "That's what you think. We're suing you for wrongful death. You won't be able to afford a funeral for a goldfish by the time we're done with you."

Larry's mouth dropped open.

Vanna crept up next to her brother with an apologetic smile. "Can't we put everything on hold until we find out what happened to Mom?" She blinked a lot.

"It doesn't matter," Vander said. "Either he killed Mom himself, or he caused it to happen somehow. He was in the house while she was dying, and he didn't do anything to help!"

"Legally speaking—" Clarence only got out a couple of words.

"Your mother was a monster!" Arnold's nostrils flared and he made sweeping gestures with his arms. "If she wasn't dead, she'd be going to jail. Now I see you two are monsters as well."

Vander swung around and got in Arnold's face. Arnold did not back down from the snarling younger man. Clarence pushed in front of me to get beside Arnold. Angry voices rose, too many to make out any words.

Finally, the funeral director squeezed through the door. "People! That's quite enough." He might normally speak in a low, gentle tone, but he knew how to project as well. Maybe scenes like this weren't as unusual as one might hope.

"Out." He grabbed Vander's arm in one hand and Arnold's in the other. "All of you, out. I want to see you heading directly to your separate cars, or I'll call the police."

I scurried around them to the door and opened it with my shoulder, waving Clarence and Vanna forward as I stepped through. Who knew what would happen when the funeral director released Arnold and Vander? He might have embarrassed them enough to behave, but I didn't want to count on it.

"Sorry," Vanna whispered. "He's upset." She ran after her brother, grabbed his arm, and dragged him through the parking lot. They got in a dark blue sedan.

Arnold shook off the funeral director's hand and glanced at me. "Hey, I didn't start it."

"Well done. You want a gold star?" I smiled at the funeral director. "Thanks. We can take it from here."

He looked at the three of us remaining. "If there are legal questions about who makes the arrangements . . ."

"I think Mr. Hodge only wants to know his options right now," I said. "Consider this a preliminary visit and don't make any firm plans yet."

He nodded, shook his head, and hurried back into the

building.

I tapped my foot and glared at Arnold.

He spread his hands wide. "Hey, I only told the truth. Honesty is the best policy."

Clarence pressed the heel of his hand to his forehead. "Maybe you should try the second-best policy for a while."

"Very funny," I said. "I didn't realize how much work it would be wrangling my old farts brigade."

Arnold drew himself up indignantly. "Coffee Shop Irregulars."

"Irregular is right. As in erratic, capricious, and unreliable."

The blue sedan drove out of the parking lot. At least Pamela's children had vacated the field of battle after their bombshell.

"What do you think about this wrongful death claim?" I asked.

"They'll have a hard time winning, unless they can get a jury to believe Larry actually killed Pamela," Clarence said.

"Which they won't." Arnold snorted. "It's an attempt to get money, nothing more. Just like their mother. *They* probably killed her."

Could Vander and Vanna have planned things like this all along? Did they get rid of their mother, planning to sue Larry?

That went beyond unlikely all the way to unfathomable. It might make sense to kill Larry and let their mother inherit. If they didn't want to share with Pamela, they could get rid of her later.

But Pamela was dead, and Larry hadn't been injured.

Even if they proved Larry killed their mother, they might not get a hold of his money, not when his children were around to fight for it. And if they wanted to set up Larry as a murderer, they could've done a better job of it. They wouldn't have broken the window and stolen a few items if they wanted to make it look like Larry had killed his wife.

"I guess we should go," Clarence said.

"Yeah. I'm sure Larry appreciated seeing you." At least at first.

"Is there anything we can do to help with the murder investigation?" Arnold asked.

"Avoid getting in fights?" I smiled to take away a little of the sting. He meant well. "Other than that, I'm not sure. Maybe ask your legal contacts about this wrongful death suit. Is there anything we need to do about it right away? Can Diamond handle that, or do we need another lawyer?"

Actually, I assumed anything legal like that would take weeks if not months to get going, and that was if Vander wasn't merely making empty threats hoping for a handout. But if the task kept Clarence and Arnold out of trouble and made them feel useful, that made my day easier.

They agreed and headed for their car. I sat on a bench outside the funeral home and closed my eyes, enjoying the sun on my face. So much for asking Vander and Vanna more questions. My "assistants" might turn out to be more trouble than they were worth. On the other hand, I could hardly blame Arnold for being mad. Larry had just been released from the hospital and had lost his wife. His and Pamela's children should be comforting each other and working together to take care of matters. Too bad so many people got overwrought after a loved one's death and made matters worse.

My phone rang. Speaking of assistants, it was Marty. "I haven't found Pamela on a dating site. If she was on one, she shut down her account. Can Joe and I do anything else?"

"I'd like to get back into Larry's house," I said. "The police have released the crime scene, and it hasn't been cleaned yet. Larry is out of the hospital, but he's going to stay at the hotel with his kids for a few days. Maybe he'll give me a key."

"What are you hoping to find?" Marty asked.

"I'm not sure. I'd like to see the crime scene for myself." Maybe something would offer a suggestion. Or maybe I was getting desperate. "Other than that, we're still hoping to find something in Pamela's past that suggests why someone would want to kill her. Since we didn't turn up anything on social media or by asking the neighbors, our only hope is to find evidence where she lived."

"Joe and I can help you search," Marty said.

"I'll text you if I get a key and let you know when we'll be there." I had mixed feelings about bringing other people along, given how the last hour had gone, but maybe one of them would pick up on something I missed, and a search of the house would go faster with several people.

I hung up and checked the time. I had a few hours before I needed to meet Jen, Mackenzie, and Carly at the climbing gym. Maybe I should see about getting a key now and getting to Larry's house.

Vanna and Vander had declared war. Did they have a key to the house? They couldn't manipulate the crime scene now, because the police already had their photos and other records. Could they do other damage? Change computer passwords, freeze accounts, remove valuables?

Remove evidence of what might have gotten their mother killed? Surely they wanted their mother's murderer caught—unless they felt it was more important to get Larry's money.

Yeah, I should definitely get over there ASAP. And maybe see about getting Larry's locks changed.

Chapter Fifteen

LARRY DIDN'T ACTUALLY have a key to his house, because it used a keyless door lock with a touchpad. Good thing, since he'd been taken to the hospital in his pajamas. He gave me a guest code and I headed for his house.

Marty, Joe, and Mackenzie waited outside.

"I thought you had finals coming up," I told Mackenzie.

"We're doing a group project. My three partners spent most of the semester complaining because I blow the curve, and now they've latched on to me hoping I'll do all the work and they'll get a good grade." Her smile turned a bit wicked. "I'm practicing my leadership by assigning them tasks. Once they're done, and only then, I'll put the whole thing together and proof it."

"Nice. Well, glad to have you along. Larry didn't ask too many questions about why I wanted into the house, so I kept it vague. I didn't want to ask for his computer password in case he got uncomfortable with the idea of us investigating Pamela."

"We're trying to help him," Joe said.

"Yes, but his feelings about her are ... complex right now, since she's dead."

"Bet you I can get in their computer within ten

minutes," Mackenzie said. "Either they won't have a password, or it's something simple, or it's written down within view of the computer. Possibly both of the last two."

"Hey now," Joe said. "We're not all dinosaurs just because we're old."

Mackenzie linked her arm through his. "As long as you don't think computers get tired from a hard drive."

We headed up the walk. Mac continued, "It's not age-based, or not entirely. About a quarter of American adults use easy passwords like 'one-two-three-four-five-six' or all ones or 'password.' A whole bunch more use their own name, a family member's name, their pet's name, or their birthdate."

"Let's hope Larry and Pamela are among them," Marty said.

I studied the door keypad, making sure I understood the sequence to get in. I couldn't believe I hadn't noticed it when I was there before. I'd gotten sloppy.

I looked up and saw the door cam in a high corner. Yeah, my hiking hat would have hidden my face at that angle. The police probably hadn't tried too hard to track me down, since I hadn't gone inside and I didn't fit the profile of the known burglar.

I pushed the door open. We clustered right outside the doorway peeking in. It didn't look like a crime scene. I knew better than to expect a chalk outline of the body or crime scene tape draped all over the place like streamers. Still, the fact that this looked like an ordinary house was almost creepier. We were stepping into a place where someone had recently died a violent death. It wasn't the first time for me, but I still got a chill. I didn't believe in ghosts, but the idea of a spirit lingering where it had unfinished business made a little too much sense. If someone murdered me, I'd want to stick around to make sure they got caught.

Noise came from around the corner, a kind of grinding motor sound.

Marty gasped. Joe rushed into the house. He swung around the corner out of our sight.

Someone screamed, a female voice.

I stumbled as Marty and Mackenzie pushed past me to get through the doorway. I grabbed the doorframe, caught my balance, and went through after them.

From the foyer, I could see through the living room to where Joe stood outside Larry's office with his hand pressed to his chest. "It's you," he said.

"Who are you?" The woman's voice wavered, high-pitched with nerves but still familiar.

I squeezed past Mackenzie and Marty to see into the office. "Wendy."

She blinked at me. "I have Dad's permission to be here." She gave her head a quick shake, perhaps recognizing how defensive that sounded. "What are you doing here? Who are these people?"

"We have your dad's permission as well," I said. "I thought you and your brother were at the hotel today."

"I just stopped by to . . . deal with a few things." Her left hand clenched papers, holding them in front of her body like a shield. She jerked her hand down and tried to hide the papers behind herself.

I walked closer. She stood by a paper shredder. It was

silent now but could have produced the grinding sound. I pried the papers from her hand. Torn edges around the staple showed where some pages had already been ripped out.

I studied the first page. "A will? Larry's will?"

"He left everything to her!"

"You know, his lawyer has a copy of the will on file," Joe said. "It hardly matters now anyway, with Pamela dead."

Wendy threw herself into the office chair and crossed her arms. "I know. I was just angry. It's not fair!"

"Oh, honey," Marty said. "Fair or not, it was his choice. You cut off your father when he married Pamela, stopped talking to him, right?"

"Yes, but only to make a point. It wouldn't have been forever." Wendy covered her face with her hands and groaned. "This is all such a mess." She dropped her hands to her lap. "We had these plans, Heath and me, for how we were going to handle this week. And then we got here, and everything's changed, and . . . I guess I just wanted to do *something*."

"Surely you could find something more productive than destroying your father's papers," Marty said.

"I already cleaned up the mess." Her face scrunched up and she shivered. "It wasn't bad, really—I've faced worse messes when my kids were sick—but to see someone's blood where they died. Her blood. Yuck. But I also couldn't help feeling sorry for her."

So much for getting clues from the crime scene. I doubted we'd spot anything there the police had missed, but we might have learned something the police were keeping secret.

Now what?

Mackenzie stood in a corner, blending in with the background. She met my gaze and shrugged.

"He'll be grateful for you cleaning," Marty said. "Why don't you go back to the hotel now? Your father will be finished at the funeral home soon. Take this time to reconnect with him. You've all been through a lot lately. You need each other now."

Marty escorted Wendy to the door. In the office, Joe frowned. "We've met that girl half a dozen times. I can't blame her for being scared when she first saw me, but she didn't seem to recognize us at all."

Mackenzie patted his shoulder. "You old folks all look alike."

"You mean handsome?"

"Right, sure." She dropped into the computer chair, tipped up the keyboard, and pulled out a slip of paper. "See, passwords. Hacking isn't even challenging anymore. At least when people write down their passwords and leave them at the computer, they're not exposed to people halfway around the world. Am I trying to find anything in particular?"

"Anything from Pamela's past that might explain why someone would want to attack her," I said. "Did she have threatening emails from someone? If you can access financial documents, was she moving large amounts of money? Larry said they only have the one computer, so if she was online at all, it would be here."

Marty came back. "Poor girl."

"Idiot girl," Joe said. "Doesn't look good, her trying to destroy Larry's most recent will."

"It doesn't," I said, "but I can't see how she'd benefit from doing it, other than venting her frustration."

I looked through the pages of the will that remained. It was mostly legalese. I couldn't tell if Larry had specified what would happen if Pamela died before he did. If he'd left his money to charity in that case, the will would still have applied, and destroying it could have helped Wendy and Heath, if they'd actually managed to destroy every copy, and if a previous will had favored them, and if Larry died before making yet another will. Lots of ifs.

I wasn't sure where Wendy had found the will, but a drawer in the desk stood partway open. Joe knelt in front of it and flipped through the file folders. "Most of this paperwork is several years old. Records from the purchase of this house and his car, social security documents."

The top of Larry's desk was fairly clean, except for a couple of receipts. I took a closer look at them.

"That's odd. This receipt is from a restaurant in the Los Angeles airport a couple of days ago. The day Heath flew in. Wendy might have arrived that day too, but surely she wouldn't go through Los Angeles."

"What's it doing here?" Joe asked.

"That's what makes it odd," I said. "I didn't think Heath had been here yet. The police only just released the house, so if he isn't here now with Wendy, did he sneak in when it was a closed crime scene? Was he here the day Pamela died?"

"Want me to call and ask him?" Marty pulled out her phone. "I have the kids' numbers."

"Sure. I'm going to search the rest of the house." I left everyone else in the office. The police were looking for an outside intruder or else evidence that Larry had killed his wife. They wouldn't bother with a thorough search of every nook and cranny in the house. That's where we might have an advantage.

In the living room, I paused to look for places that might hide documents. I flipped through the magazines in a magazine rack. No bookcase, so I didn't have to search through books. I doubted many people hid things in books, and I was confident this recently built house in the suburbs wouldn't have secret latches to swing back bookcases and reveal hidden rooms. Still, I was getting desperate for a clue.

I did a similar quick search of the bedroom. The covers on the bed were rumpled where Larry had been sleeping. The nightstand on that side held reading glasses, a box of tissues, an alarm clock, and a few other items in a drawer. The nightstand on the other side was empty. Had Pamela even slept in this room?

In the master bathroom with walk-in closet, I found only the clothing and toiletries you might expect. The labels on the medicine said who they were for and the prescribing doctors. Pamela's sedatives were from a different doctor than all the others. I looked up his name on my phone. His website made it sound like getting antidepressants and pain killers was a breeze. He sounded like the kind of guy who used to hand out medical marijuana prescriptions and now had to make up for the loss in business since Arizona legalized marijuana.

I passed back through the living room to the other side of the house and found the bedroom Pamela must have used. The bed was smaller and had two pillows stacked one on the other. A dresser and nightstand in there didn't turn up anything unusual. She was apparently choosing not to sleep with her husband, although she did use the master bathroom and large closet. I didn't find evidence that she shared the room with anyone else, so at least she wasn't drugging Larry and cheating on him in his own house.

The room that had been Betty's sewing room, according to what Joe had said the day we kidnapped Larry, looked like no one had entered it in months, perhaps years. Her sewing machine still stood on a long table by the windows that looked out over the golf course.

One of those windows was broken. Shards of glass still stuck to the edges of the frame. If a burglar came in through that window, they would've left fiber fragments—or blood—on the glass shards and disturbed more of the dust on the table. No wonder the police thought the broken window might be a ruse.

Assuming the window hadn't been broken in an unrelated accident, at least the so-called burglar had been smart enough to break the window from the outside, so the glass fell inward, but they needed to go a couple of steps further to make it look believable.

Maybe a burglar broke the window, and then thought to go around the house and try the back door.

I shook my head. It was hard to overestimate the stupidity people could achieve, but that was a stretch.

Marty paused in the doorway. "Anything yet?"

I explained my thoughts on the broken window. "I didn't notice it when we passed by the other day. I'd like to believe that means it wasn't broken then. However, I didn't notice the door keypad or camera either."

"You were all distracted that day."

"True. Did you reach Heath?"

"He says he hasn't been to the house, so someone must have stolen the receipts from his pocket. They were in his jacket, which he wore to the hospital to see Larry. He hasn't gone many other places."

"Do you believe him?"

We walked back toward the office as Marty answered. "I can't say for sure. He seemed genuinely puzzled, and then angry, about the receipts. Could someone have planted them here to make it look like he'd been here?"

"I suppose." I stepped into the office. "Someone might have wanted it to look like Heath had been here in the morning, before Pamela died. But it wouldn't have done much good unless the person had gotten the receipts here before the police did their search. In that case, surely the police would have bagged the receipts as evidence."

Vander or Vanna could have stolen Heath's receipts at the hospital. So could Wendy. I could have, my father could have, any of Larry's other visitors might have been able to—had Clarence and Arnold been there? A stranger might have managed it. Heath could be lying.

I squeezed my temples. This case was bizarre. "Everyone is acting suspiciously, but they aren't doing things that actually make sense if they're trying to cover up a murder."

"People don't always act rationally at the best of times," Marty said. "After a death? Even when someone dies peacefully and it's expected, family members can go kind of crazy in their grief. Old resentments come out. Sisters who always got along are suddenly fighting over objects that aren't worth anything. Maybe people find it easier to be angry than to be sad."

"I guess, but that doesn't help us," I said. "Mackenzie, please tell me you found something."

"Someone tried to get into Larry's investment accounts several times in the last month but failed."

"Okay. What do you think that means?" I asked.

She spun the chair around and grinned at me. "Someone isn't as good with computers as I am."

"Remind me to keep that girl away from our computer." Joe got to his feet and shook out his legs. "I didn't find anything in the files that helps us."

"Mackenzie, you found Larry's computer password, but not his account passwords?" I asked.

"I found those too, but they were in a computer folder labeled Health. He had another folder labeled Financial, which had tax info but not the passwords. Props to Larry for not having the document labeled Passwords and sitting in his main folder. He at least hid them *a little*. They were real passwords too, maybe because the financial sites are more likely to insist on a strong password."

"So the attempt to get into his accounts came from this computer, right, not from outside?" I asked.

Mac nodded. "Best guess, Pamela tried to get into Larry's accounts when Larry was out of it, but either he wouldn't give her his password, or he couldn't remember it in his drugged state, and she couldn't figure it out."

"I guess that makes as much sense as anything," I said.

"Does any of this help?" Marty asked.

"Darned if I know."

I had a better picture of the way Larry and Pamela had lived, and more evidence that Pamela had married Larry to get his money rather than to be his wife.

"The problem is, we keep finding evidence against Pamela, and we don't need that," I said. "We'd be all set if we had to prove Pamela had been abusing Larry, but that's no longer the problem. To solve her murder, we need evidence against her kids, or Larry's children, or someone from Pamela's past, or the neighborhood burglar."

"I hope the police are doing better than we are," Joe said. "Otherwise they'll definitely be tempted to blame this on Larry."

Evidence against Larry would at least give us answers, but if he'd knocked her down and couldn't remember it, what evidence could we find?

"Cheer up," Marty said. "They might decide to blame it on the nameless burglar and let the whole thing fade out. Then we only have to deal with Larry never having answers."

"And wondering if he really did kill her," Joe said.

We stood in morose silence for a minute.

"I wonder what the police know," Joe said.

"Maybe it's time to find out." I'd been avoiding the police on this case, because I didn't want to waste time getting bogged down in lengthy explanations about our activities the day of Pamela's death. But if the police were making progress—progress that pointed away from Larry—we could take a break. Even if they weren't, maybe they had some evidence that would lead to an answer, and we might be able to take shortcuts getting there that the police couldn't take.

"Do you think the police will tell you anything?" Joe asked.

"Not those guys who visited us, Quarterman and Olabarria, but Detective Padilla might."

I'd helped the detective put away one murderer already, and I thought she trusted me. She might be able to find out what the police had in Pamela's murder, and she might be willing to share.

Might be. No guarantee.

Mackenzie's phone beeped. "Uh-oh." She looked at me. "That's my reminder that it's time to head to our next . . . appointment."

"What are you two girls up to?" Marty asked.

I didn't want to explain the whole situation with Todd, the developer, and the city council member, so I just said, "Jen convinced us to try a rock climbing gym."

Marty glanced at my cane. "Are you sure that's a good idea?"

"No, but we're doing it anyway."

Chapter Sixteen

I MADE AN appointment with Detective Padilla and headed for the climbing gym. I found a parking space and took a lap around the lot to loosen up my stiff leg. As I headed inside, a young teen boy looked at my cane and then my face with an incredulous expression. He nudged his friend and laughed.

I was tempted to whack him with my cane. Instead, I quietly stepped up to the counter to pay and get my equipment. Look at me pretending to be all mature.

By the time I walked into the main room juggling a harness, climbing shoes, and my cane, Jen, Mackenzie, and Carly had already suited up in their rented climbing harnesses.

A young woman with olive skin and dark brown dreadlocks turned to me. Her name tag said Genesis. "Do you need help putting on your harness?"

I lifted my cane. "First of all, tell me, am I foolish to even try this?"

"Not at all. Some amputees climb. Even people in wheelchairs. Ideally, rock climbers use their legs more than their arms." She gestured at her own muscular legs. "For most of us, our legs are stronger, so you last longer if you can hold on loosely with your hands and use the power in your legs. But there are disabled people who climb using only upper body strength."

I managed a chuckle. "I'm not sure how much of that I have either."

Her smile revealed a cute little gap between her front teeth. "Well, today you'll find out. Don't worry, we'll start you on the easiest wall, where it slopes slightly away from you. I take it you can put weight on both legs."

"Yes, but the left one isn't strong, and it tires easily."

She pointed to a bench along the wall. "Have a seat, and I'll help you get the harness on. You'll be fine but let me know if you're in pain or struggling and we'll find a way to handle it."

Darn it. I was kind of hoping she'd tell me to sit out today.

She crouched in front of me and held the harness while I got my legs through the leg loops. Without her guidance, I probably would have had the harness backward, upside down, and inside out.

I stood. Genesis dragged the harness up my body and tightened the loops around my waist and legs. She grabbed the front and pulled up. "You'll be hanging from this, so make sure it's not pinching anywhere. How does it feel?"

I tugged the legs of my baggy shorts to get rid of fabric bunched up in the crotch. "Fine, I guess."

"Do you need help with your shoes?"

"No, I can manage." Her casual acceptance of people with special needs was great. That didn't mean I liked *being* a person with special needs. One day I'd have to get over it.

Once again, this was not that day.

"All right, we'll start in a few minutes. Feel free to sit until then." Genesis turned to help someone else.

The slipper-style leather shoes looked ridiculously small. I felt like one of the stepsisters trying to fit into Cinderella's shoes, but once I had them on, they were comfortable enough.

I massaged my leg and looked around. Jen and Carly stood on the mats in the middle of the room, chatting and laughing. Mackenzie leaned against the wall near the cubbyholes, holding her phone in both hands as if texting. She glanced at me and winked.

We were here to trap Eric Konietzko. Rock climbing was merely a means to that end.

Still, I felt light-headed and a little queasy, and that wasn't because of dealing with a shady politician. I had been going to physical therapy, doing the exercises at home, and pushing myself to walk a little farther than comfortable each day. However, the injury was too new for me to get ambitious about returning to my former lifestyle, let alone trying new things that were physically demanding.

I studied the room. Climbing walls had been built within the structural walls. The climbing walls sometimes angled away from the climber. At other times, they sloped toward the climber or even curved overhead. Colorful holds in different shapes and sizes were scattered across all the walls.

People mostly seemed to be in pairs, one climbing and one standing at the base of the wall handling the safety rope attached to the climber. When someone reached the top, they sat back in their harness and their partner lowered them down.

One section had a low cave. In there, the climbers didn't use ropes. If they fell, they landed on a thick pad. The drop wasn't more than five or six feet, but I wouldn't have wanted to fall that far and land on my back. The cave echoed with grunts of effort and yells of encouragement.

In the main part of the room, where people climbed higher, backed up by ropes, several athletic-looking men and women were hauling themselves up the walls—no, more like *dancing* up the walls—at an astonishing pace. Clearly they weren't in the beginning class.

A young man had made it up the straight wall to a section of holds that actually stretched onto the ceiling. He had his toes hooked into a couple of the colorful holds bolted to the walls, his hands gripping additional holds. He reached for the next one.

He dropped straight down.

I gasped.

The rope attached to his harness stopped him about eight feet below the ceiling. He swung and spun and swore. I didn't recognize the words or the language, but I knew swearing when I heard it.

His partner on the ground laughed, called up to him, and started letting him down. He landed, shook out his arms, and the two men switched places.

I'd known he was on a rope. I knew, in theory, what happened when someone came off the wall. That didn't make the fall easier to witness. I suspected it wouldn't make it easier when it happened to me.

A woman with lean, muscular limbs moved smoothly

between colored holds that looked about the size of grapes, her arms and legs out like a spider. At the top of the wall, she tapped a taped mark, called "Take," and sat back, looking as comfortable hanging in her harness as if seated on a swing set. She turned to call down to the partner lowering her. The climber had a weathered face and streaks of gray in her brown hair. Some of these athletes weren't so young after all. Youth predominated, but it didn't own the place.

I'd hiked mountains and traveled rough terrain to get a good story. A decade ago, I would have loved trying something like this. It looked like I had neither age nor injury as excuses to avoid it now.

I tried to think of another excuse.

Someone stopped in front of me, blocking my view. I glanced up at Jen. She jerked her head to call my attention to Carly and the man now with her. So this was Eric Konietzko. He wore chinos and a lightweight sports jacket. I couldn't hear them, but Carly's posture was taunting while Eric's was defensive.

"Get up," Jen said. "Walk over that way."

"I don't want to meet him yet," I said. "I might need to approach him later."

"A guy like that doesn't notice women over forty. Just walk past and make sure he sees your cane. Carly needs reinforcement to show that anyone can do this. I guarantee he won't remember you later."

Anyone could do this, even me, an aging woman with a limp. Oh well, I'd pretended to be worse things in pursuit of a story, and this wasn't even pretend. If a guy was foolish enough to give in to pressure to do something he didn't want to do because an older woman could do it, he deserved to suffer.

I crossed the room, making sure I was within Eric's view but keeping my face turned away from him. I might have limped a little more than absolutely necessary.

I paused in front of the wall and pretended to study the holds for a few seconds. When I glanced back over my shoulder, Eric was heading toward the entrance hall. Had we failed?

Carly turned and shot me a grin and a thumbs-up.

Eric must be going to rent equipment. Excellent.

A minute later, Genesis called the beginning class to gather around her. Eric was still trying to get into his harness. Carly helped. I wandered a bit closer to them.

"You'd better take your phone out of your pocket and leave it in a cubbyhole," Carly said. "I know, I know. You're so important you can't miss a call. But you wouldn't want to hit your phone against one of the holds and break it."

Eric grumbled but stuck his phone into a cubby, hiding it under his jacket. Mackenzie, leaning against the wall nearby, didn't glance up from her phone, but I knew she'd noted where he put his things.

Genesis explained the basics of climbing in a gym and went over safety rules.

Eric kept glancing toward the cubbies. "I can't believe you talked me into this," he muttered to Carly. "I'm too busy for this nonsense. If I miss an important call . . ."

"If it's that important, they'll call back." She nudged him. "Now pay attention or you'll miss something that might truly be life or death."

He turned back toward Genesis with a hearty sigh.

I shifted to stand behind him, so if he did turn, I might block his view of the cubbies. That meant I couldn't see when Mackenzie got his phone. I trusted her to take care of that end of things. I didn't want to miss the safety info either.

Genesis and a couple of assistants paired us up and pointed us toward the belay stations embedded in the floor along the climbing wall. Genesis took Jen and me to a section of the wall that was sloped away from us. Not so much that you could tell unless you saw it up close, but any amount of sloped away was better than straight up or overhanging.

"Feel free to use any holds on the wall if you want, but see the pieces of green tape next to some of the holds? They mark the easiest route. You'll have nice, big holds, and each one should be within easy reach."

Big was relative, but these holds ranged from palm-sized to weird shapes eight or ten inches across. Other parts of the wall had tiny holes you could only pinch between a few fingers.

I glanced back toward the cubbyholes. No sign of Mackenzie. She must have gone into the bathroom or outside to work on Eric's phone. As long as Carly kept him distracted, we'd be fine—assuming Mackenzie could get into Eric's phone with her fake fingerprint.

I gave my attention to climbing. We practiced using the belay equipment. Genesis assured us that if the belayer panicked and let go, the unit would automatically lock, holding the climber in place.

Jen climbed first. Once she was a few feet up, she sat back in her harness with her feet braced on the wall in front of her. I used the belay device to let her down slowly.

"Great," Genesis said. "Ready to try it for real?"

Jen nodded rapidly, her smile lighting up the room.

"You comfortable with belaying?" Genesis asked me.

I gave a casual shrug. "She's my sister, so if I drop her, it's no great loss."

Jen punched me in the arm. I assured Genesis that I was ready, and Jen started up the wall. She made it look easy. I wanted to believe that meant it actually was easy, but Jen was in pretty good shape. It probably took me longer to let her down than it took her to get up.

We switched places. Genesis checked that Jen was using the belay system properly and I was hooked onto the other end of the rope.

"Better let me take your cane," Genesis said. "Don't want to leave it on the floor and have someone stumble on it."

My fingers tightened on the cane in refusal. I couldn't climb with it, I hated having to use it, but I didn't want anyone to take it away. I held it out and forced my hand to let go. She trotted over to the cubbies and leaned the cane against one side. Mackenzie strolled out of the restroom and glanced toward us.

I looked around for Eric Konietzko. He was about ten feet up the wall, all his attention focused on the climb.

Mackenzie slipped the phone back into Eric's cubby as Genesis returned to Jen and me. Operation spy phone complete. Now we merely had to get through the actual climbing.

I remind myself to breathe. You'd think after nearly fifty years, that wouldn't require conscious thought.

Okay. Right hand on a hold. Easy enough, since my feet were still on the ground. Left hand on a hold.

Now I had to step up. Only if I did that, my hands would be too low, chest height. I didn't think I had the upper body strength to hold on like that. So first, move my hands to higher holds, above my head. Yes, that made sense. Then when I stepped up onto the first two footholds, my hands were up by my face. Not too awkward.

Once I got started, Genesis murmured suggestions, tapping good holds for my feet and recommending that I turn my feet out to use the side rather than the toes. That did feel more stable, even if my left leg complained at the unusual position. As a bonus, turning my feet outward kept me from banging my knees into other holds.

The handholds here were big enough to get a decent grip. It really wasn't that bad.

I paused to catch my breath. Must have been forgetting to breathe again.

Eric hadn't moved. The young man helping him and Carly gave instructions for where to reach next, but Eric appeared immobilized.

His fear of heights must've kicked in. He was stuck. Only ten feet off the ground and supported by a rope, yet he was afraid of falling.

I looked down. I was higher than he was. My feet were probably fifteen feet above the ground, which put my eyes close to twenty feet up. Too far.

I gripped the holds tighter. My arms ached. My fingers stung. Genesis had said something about "holding on loosely." That seemed impossible.

I saw myself falling, plummeting, hitting the ground, landing on my bad leg. Rolling as a car sped past, so close I could feel the air swirling in its wake. Lying on the ground, my leg throbbing, blood everywhere, the explosion echoing in my ears but not loud enough to drown out the shrieks from people injured and dying.

No no no no no.

Chapter Seventeen

I CLUNG TO reality. I wasn't back in the Middle East after a bomb had exploded. I wasn't on the street in Arizona, diving out of the way of a car driven by a mysterious attacker, as I'd done a few weeks earlier.

I stared at the wall in front of me, the texture of the white-painted plywood, the red of the blobby hold under my hand—red like pooling blood—

I switched my gaze to the hold under my other hand, a nice dark blue in a shape kind of like a smile. I concentrated on the rough texture under my hands, the aching of my fingers, the tension in my arm muscles, even the tremor in my bad leg. I sipped a few shallow breaths.

Breathing got easier. I could force my chest to move enough to draw in deeper breaths.

Breathe in, breathe out. In and out.

The waves of dizziness receded. My stomach settled. I was firmly back in the climbing gym, on a safety rope, with my sister waiting at the other end. I was halfway up the wall, holding the cheerfully colorful handholds, with my cane far away across the room. But at least I was here, in the present.

I wanted down. I could tell Jen to "take" so she'd take up any slack in the rope, making it tighter. I could sit back in my harness, and she'd lower me down. She might prod me to try again, to go a few more moves, but if I insisted, she'd bring me down. She might not even tease me too much about it afterward.

I took another deep breath and blew it out slowly. I commanded my arms and hands to relax—not all the way, but enough that the trembling ache receded. I moved my right arm up a foot to a green hold shaped like a cartoon ghost. My left hand went to a smaller red blob. My fingers slid over the hold and tucked into a nice pocket on the back. I'd had no idea that was there until my fingers found it. My grip felt secure. What a nice surprise.

Next I had to move my feet. I didn't want to look down, so I felt around with my right foot until I found something at knee height that provided enough of a ledge for the ball of my foot. I shifted my weight onto that foot, pulled with my arms, and stood up on that hold. I found a place to rest my left foot.

I was doing it, moving up, not down. Forward, not backward. This was probably a good metaphor, but I didn't have the brain space to pursue it.

The next set of moves went easier. By the one after that, I could glance down toward my knees, focusing on the wall, to find footholds.

Finally I got high enough to tap the ceiling. I had to stretch my arm to the absolute extent of my reach, but hey, that counted.

"Okay," I yelled down, and then remembered the correct term, "Take."

The rope tightened and my harness squeezed my legs. I

slowly, slowly eased back until my weight was mainly in the harness. I cautiously loosened one hand. When the harness and rope held me securely, I let go with the other arm.

Jen called up, "Ready?"

"Down please."

I dropped a foot or so with a jerk. I gasped and wrapped my hands around the rope in front of my chest. Logically, I knew holding the rope right above my harness wouldn't keep me from falling if something went wrong—I could hardly hold myself up in the air—but my hands didn't seem to get the message.

Jen found a rhythm and lowered me more smoothly. I concentrated on keeping my feet out in front of me, spread wide so I didn't twist to the right or left, walking down the wall.

I reached the ground. My legs threatened to collapse. Both of them.

Genesis put an arm around me, holding me steady. "You did it!"

"I did it." My voice sounded hoarse. My whole body trembled. My legs shook with fatigue, and not only the damaged one.

She handed me the cane. "Do you need to take a break?"

"Yeah, I think so."

I glanced around as if coming out of a dream, the world suddenly filled with more noise and movement. Eric Konietzko sat on the ground, his arms folded around his bent knees, his head down. It was hard to feel sorry for a man like him, but I almost managed it.

Carly caught me watching and rolled her eyes.

"Tell you what," I said to Jen, "why don't you and Carly pair up? I'm glad I tried this, but I think it was enough for one day. It looks like Carly needs a new partner too."

"That might work." Genesis crossed to Eric and crouched beside him.

Jen took my arm. "Are you okay? Was it too much? I want to—but I didn't mean to—"

"I know. It's okay that you pushed me. It's up to me to decide when it's enough, or too much. I can see doing this again someday." I was almost surprised to hear myself say that, but it was true. "Maybe in a couple of months, when my leg is stronger." And when the PTSD had faded a little, if it ever did. No guarantee there, but I could hope.

Jen joined Carly. I dragged myself across the room, which now seemed much larger than the thirty feet it actually was. I sat on the bench next to Mackenzie, who still had her phone out.

"We good?" I murmured.

"All set. I'm looking in his phone now."

We were silent for a minute as Eric came over. He wrestled with his harness as if trying to escape a boa constrictor, kicked off the climbing shoes, grabbed his stuff, and rushed out of the building without even bothering to return his gear to the counter.

"I wonder if Carly enjoyed seeing him like that," Mackenzie said.

"She didn't look sympathetic. That's probably just as well, if he's the criminal we think he is. We don't need her softening toward him."

"Yeah. If he's been taking bribes for political favors, he

deserves to be caught and brought to justice." Mackenzie chewed on her lip for a second. "It's weird seeing people like that as human."

"Technically, he is human."

"You know what I mean. Vulnerable."

"That's part of being human," I said. "We all have strengths and weaknesses, good qualities and flaws. You can sympathize with someone's frailty and still hold them accountable for their actions."

"Yeah. Anyway, I'll start going through his email and other accounts. I can see who he called, but unless they left a voice mail and he hasn't deleted it, I don't know what was said."

"Let me know what you find."

For a minute we watched the climbers. "Mac, does it bother you, the things we ask you to do? I know we joke about you being a hacker, but as far as I know, you were law-abiding before you met me."

"Well . . . moderately law-abiding. Let's say I don't think I committed any felonies previous to our acquaintance. I wish we had another way to do this legally. But I understand the challenges."

"The law works so slowly sometimes," I said. "It gives people too much time to hide their tracks or leave the country, and that's assuming you can get the law to pay attention in the first place. Pamela's murder is one thing. The police will definitely investigate, although that doesn't mean they'll find and put away the killer. It's another thing that we suspect a politician is taking bribes, but we have no evidence to support it. The police can't subpoena his records based on a random tip, and they shouldn't, or it would be too easy for people to harass each other with false claims."

"If we do find evidence, can the police use it?"

"Yep. Evidence found by private citizens acting on their own is usually admissible in court. The private citizen is still liable for crimes committed in order to get the evidence, but if I pass along info saying it came from a secret informant, I can't imagine they'd bother to pursue you."

"That's good. Well, if I don't find anything, no harm done, I guess." She squirmed on the bench. "It's not like I'd want someone looking through my email, poking around in my online search history, but I won't do anything with what we find, unless we find evidence of illegal activity. I guess I can live with that."

I tried to remember how I felt about such things in my early twenties. On the one hand, I'd been more idealistic way back then. On the other, I was in journalism, not law enforcement. I believed the truth could set you free or put you in prison if that was where you belonged. Nothing mattered more than revealing the truth. Reporters had a duty to uncover it.

That didn't mean we had no principles. Journalists often debated moral guidelines, and the Society of Professional Journalists had an official code of ethics. Still, that didn't prevent more aggressive reporters from searching people's papers if they got the chance or listening in on conversations or lying to people. People lied all the time in daily life. The police could legally lie to suspects, claiming a criminal's partner had provided evidence against them, or saying the police would ask the judge to go easy on a suspect who cooperated, when the police actually had no influence. The world worked that way, with subterfuge and manipulation.

But sometimes I wished it didn't. Maybe it was time for me to review the journalism code of ethics to see how far I'd strayed from that path.

Chapter Eighteen

BY THE TIME I got home, I wanted to throw myself into bed and sleep for a week. Unfortunately, my bed was upstairs, and I didn't think I could make it there without crawling. Instead, I collapsed on the couch with a groan.

Dad came out of the kitchen. "You're back. How was the climbing gym?"

"Let's just say I've proven something. I'm not old enough to know better."

"Good to learn. Can I get you anything?"

"Will you put on a pot of coffee? Detective Padilla is coming by soon."

I needed a shower, but the shower was also upstairs, and if I hauled myself up there, I wasn't coming down again before morning at the earliest. I'd have to hope the detective didn't have an acute sense of smell.

Dad came back with a glass of water and some ibuprofen. "Coffee's brewing."

"Thanks." I didn't realize how thirsty I was until I started drinking. "Did anything happen I should know about?"

"I don't think so. Joe called Diamond to warn her about Vander's threat of a wrongful death suit. She said it might be merely a threat, so don't worry about it until he makes another move."

Dad sat in the easy chair. He looked as fatigued as I felt. His exhaustion was probably more emotional though.

Right, because I hadn't been emotional *at all* that day.

"Larry wore out pretty quickly," Dad said. "We didn't make any final decisions, but I think today helped him start the process of accepting that Pamela is gone. I left him with his children at the hotel. They have a chance to rebuild their relationship. I hope they don't screw it up."

Dad ran his hands up his face and over his head. "Larry still isn't back to his old self. It's too early to say if it's the lingering effects of the drugs, not to mention almost no activity in the last few months—he's definitely weaker, physically—or if it's the shock of everything that's happened, or something worse."

Dad knew from experience how quickly someone could go from mentally active to showing signs of Alzheimer's or dementia.

"Marty and Joe told me what you found at Larry's house," Dad said.

"Or didn't find, mostly."

"Right. I'm trying not to worry, or to let Larry worry too much." He was silent for a minute. "That Detective Quarterman was in the hotel lobby when I came out. I think he's keeping an eye on Larry."

"He could be keeping an eye on you."

"Is that supposed to make me feel better?"

"No." I snuggled back into the corner of the sofa with my eyes closed. "I'm not sure what to do next. Maybe Detective Padilla will be able to help somehow. If we're really, really lucky, the police already have enough evidence to prosecute Pamela's murderer, and it will be someone we don't like."

"I haven't been feeling that lucky lately."

"Mmm. But we're still here."

Sometimes I had trouble being grateful that I'd survived the bombing rather than resentful that I'd torn apart my leg. Still, I knew journalists who hadn't survived the dangerous work we did, as well as colleagues who'd died suddenly of a heart attack or slowly of cancer. Survival was something to celebrate, even if it came with scars and pain.

"If your detective friend can't help, we might have to try something different," Dad said.

I opened one eye. "You have something in mind?"

"Maybe we can lure the killer out of hiding, get him or her to reveal themselves."

"Do I even want to know how you think we might do that?"

The doorbell rang.

Dad rose. "Probably not." He went to answer the door.

I greeted Yaquelin Padilla. Dad brought us coffee and slipped away. He was either giving me privacy, or he was avoiding awkward questions the detective might have about his involvement in the murder case. I suspected the latter.

Yaquelin and I chatted for a few minutes, catching up. We'd gotten friendly during my nursing home investigation, but I knew she was busy, so I didn't take long to get to the point.

"You're familiar with the Pamela Hodge murder case?"

"I'm not working it, but I looked over the files when you

said you wanted to talk about it." She quirked an eyebrow. "I see your father is a person of interest in the case."

Not a witness, but a person of interest. Interesting.

"I'd like to tell you something off the record," I said.

"Law enforcement doesn't work that way. If you tell me about involvement in a crime, I'm obligated to tell the detectives on the case."

"Okay, what if I tell you a hypothetical situation? Something that *could* have happened, and I'd like your advice in case a situation arises in the future."

"Right." She drew out the word and toasted me with her coffee mug. "Well, let's hear it."

I described the hypothetical removal of Larry from his house by his friends. "In a case such as that, the people who were there would know they didn't have anything to do with any murder that might have happened. Yet they might hesitate to tell the police about their presence, in order to avoid distractions that would lead the police away from the killer."

"I see." Padilla looked like her coffee had suddenly gone sour.

"However, say the police do not appear to be wrapping up the case quickly. Would coming forward with this information help or hinder this imaginary investigation?"

"You certainly come up with interesting theoretical narratives," Padilla said. "I thought you were a journalist, not a fiction writer."

She leaned forward, put her cup on the table, and rested her elbows on her knees.

"Okay. It would depend upon the actual specifics of the

real case, and we're only talking *hypothetically* here," she said. "If we use the Pamela Hodge murder case as an example, I don't see how your information, were it true, would help the police one way or another. That doesn't mean I recommend withholding information from the police."

"Of course not," I said. "Who would do that? So hypothetically speaking, if the murdered woman's husband got back to his house at about three thirty, and had witnesses to prove it, that wouldn't exclude him as a suspect?"

"If our imaginary victim died while her husband was at the doctor's office, that would give him an alibi. However, in the Hodge case, Ms. Hodge died close to four o'clock. They're pretty confident about that, given the body temperature. It's harder when a body has been lying around for hours, but she was found quickly. Now, she was punched in the face and hit her head. The blow to her head killed her, but probably not right away. They can estimate how long it took based on the swelling and bleeding, but it's not exact. The best guess is that she was hit between three and three thirty. Her husband might not have been home yet, or he might have arrived home, confronted her, and killed her."

Shoot. That didn't help us. I could testify that I put Larry in bed at three thirty and he seemed weak and tired, but the police might assume he was faking it and got up to confront Pamela as soon as I left.

A chill tickled my spine. Pamela might have died as I returned Larry to his bedroom. I hadn't looked in any room but the bedroom then. Or Larry could have been in the house, maybe asleep, when the killer came. Imagine knowing someone had been killed in your house while you were there.

I'd never sleep again.

"I'm afraid your guy is still a person of interest," Padilla said. "If he's not the killer himself, he could have known someone else came and is protecting them by claiming he doesn't know what happened."

"The detectives on this case don't think Larry Hodge was faking being sedated, do they?"

"His blood test showed certain levels of drugs in his bloodstream. That proves he had taken the drugs at some point, but not necessarily how much at what time, since the tests weren't taken until that evening. For all they know, he could have taken a pill after he killed Pamela to back his claim that he was asleep."

I groaned.

"I take it you don't believe Larry Hodge is a murderer," Padilla said.

"I'm working under the assumption that he isn't, but that's largely because he's a friend of my father's and we don't want him to be guilty."

"Any idea who is?"

"Not really. The lead candidates seems to be his kids or Pamela's kids, but nothing quite fits all the facts. If he's protecting someone, it's more likely to be his own children."

Padilla nodded slowly. "The police are holding back a piece of evidence that points to this being tied to the other two break-ins. But the murder of Ms. Hodge seems out of place. Home invasion leading to death isn't common. Murder at home is usually personal."

I had about given up on the idea of a burglar, but the police hadn't? But this seemed personal, and it couldn't be both. Or—

I sat up straighter. "Could it be both? Could the burglar be targeting people he knows?"

"So far we haven't found any links between the victims."

I shifted, trying to get comfortable. It didn't work. At least the aches kept me awake. "The last time we worked together, someone was committing crimes in order to obscure the crime he really wanted to commit. Could that be happening here?"

"You mean could the first two break-ins be tricks to lead us into thinking the murder of Ms. Hodge was random?"

I nodded. The previous case had been widely reported. It could even have given the murderer the idea of committing other burglaries to set up his crime.

"Anything's possible."

I couldn't tell if that meant she truly had no idea, she didn't believe it, or the police were leaning in that direction.

"Can you tell me anything else that might be helpful?" I asked.

"Off the record? This isn't for a story, right?"

"No story. I only want to help catch a murderer."

"Normally I'd tell a civilian to mind their own business."

"I like to think I'm special."

She gave a little snort and gazed at the ceiling for a minute. "When someone stages a crime so it looks different than what really happened, it's almost always someone with an intimate relationship to the victim. The person often inserts themselves into the incident in a different role."

I puzzled over that. "You mean like the killer says they witnessed the crime or pretends to find the body?"

"Exactly."

That would suggest Vanna. She couldn't have gotten from work, to her mother's house to commit a murder, and back to work again without someone noticing her absence. But if she'd come in, hit her mother on the head, and Pamela had died more quickly than the coroner thought, Vanna might have then "discovered" the body.

"However," Padilla said, "stagers make nine-one-one calls with certain unique elements. We keep those elements secret, because we don't want to make our jobs any harder than they already are. In this case, the call supports the innocence of the woman who called, Pamela Hodge's daughter."

"Okay. Vanna sounded innocent. If she killed her mother or knew her brother did it and she was supposed to discover the body later, she would've made those mistakes. But she sounded like someone truly surprised to find her mother injured."

"Right. Of the younger generation, her alibi holds up best. We know when she entered the house, and we know she called nine-one-one less than three minutes later. The medical examiner is almost certain that Pamela Hodge lay bleeding for at least half an hour, and probably longer, before she died."

"And Vanna couldn't have come earlier without being missed at work." That seemed to leave Vanna out of it.

"Larry Hodge's children, Wendy and Heath, have pretty good alibis but not one hundred percent." Padilla shrugged. "Almost any alibi can be broken if you try hard enough."

"They claim they were at the hotel all afternoon. They're

providing an alibi for each other, so if one did it, the other knew about it."

"Right. The hotel uses a system that tracks when key cards are used in a lock. Wendy's and Heath's cards show them entering their own rooms, and Heath went to the gym. The cards don't show when somebody leaves a room, so, for example, Heath could have entered the gym, immediately left, and driven to his father's house to kill his stepmother, but the timing would be tight. Neither of them took their cell phones out of the hotel. We can track that on the phones' GPS."

"They might have left their phones behind to help support the alibi."

"Maybe," Padilla said, "but most of us get so used to having our phones with us everywhere that we wouldn't even think of that. The mileage on the rental car also suggests they only went from the airport to the hotel. We haven't found a taxi or rideshare that picked up anyone during that timeframe. The staff don't remember seeing Heath or Wendy leave or enter the hotel during the time in question. It's as good an alibi as you can get, without being so perfect that the perfection makes it suspicious."

That was generally good news. It would devastate Larry if his children were convicted of murdering their stepmother. It wouldn't necessarily absolve Larry either, as some people might think the three of them had planned the crime together.

"That only leaves Vander," I said. And Arnold and Clarence, and technically my father and me, and a random stranger. No need to go into all of that.

"He has an alibi as well."

"A good one?" I asked.

"He was at an appointment. The person confirms."

"I gather you don't feel you can give me more information about the appointment."

She shifted uneasily. "I'm stretching things as is. You wouldn't want anyone talking about your medical appointments, would you?"

Ah. So Vander was with a doctor. That would seem to prove his innocence, assuming the times were accurate.

Larry had seen a doctor the day of Pamela's death. Vander also had a doctor's appointment. Pamela had been giving Larry medicine prescribed to her by a doctor, one who didn't have the best reputation. By the end of the day, Larry was in the hospital. That made for a lot of doctors.

The pieces of the puzzle shifted in my mind.

I didn't see how Larry's doctor's visit could be connected to the other elements. It had been a last-minute thing. Even Larry hadn't known about it in advance.

On the other hand, Vander's and Pamela's doctors could be connected. Pamela knew a doctor who gave prescriptions based on flimsy claims. Vander was using a doctor as his alibi.

"Pamela gave Larry sedatives prescribed for her," I said. "She got the drug from a doctor whose website advertises the ease of getting prescription narcotics. I wonder how else that doctor tries to accommodate patients. I wonder if Vander's alibi is the same doctor."

Padilla sat up straighter. "That would be interesting. I don't have an answer."

"It still leaves the question of motive," I mused. "Why would he kill his mother?"

"Anyone with a temper could kill in the heat of passion," Padilla said, "but if Vander had the presence of mind to make this look like a burglary—and especially if he committed the other two burglaries to set up a pattern—it was premeditated. I wonder how closely they examined his alibi, since he didn't seem to have anything to gain."

"He's threatening a wrongful death suit against Larry now."

Her brows drew together. "Do you think that was his plan all along?"

"It's awfully convoluted. I guess that's to his benefit, if it means we don't think he has a motive. But it's also risky. He lowers his chance of being caught for the murder, but he might lose a wrongful death suit. If that was his plan, why didn't he make it look like Larry killed Pamela? Why bother with the burglaries at all?"

"I'm baffled." She picked up her mug and drained it. "With these complicated cases, sometimes all you can do is keep pulling at the threads until something unravels. Anyone could have committed this murder physically. The killer hit Pamela on the left cheek, so they were probably right-handed, but that doesn't eliminate any of this group. The bruising suggests they didn't hit her very hard. That could indicate a weaker assailant, or it might mean the person wasn't trying to kill her or hurt her badly, or maybe they just didn't know how to throw a punch. Most people don't."

"So anyone could have the means," I said.

"Right. We're looking at motive and opportunity."

I smiled. "Hypothetically speaking, if I wanted to break Vander's alibi, I'd lean on that doctor."

Padilla put her empty coffee cup on the table and stood. "Always interesting talking to you." She gave a little salute and headed for the door.

Were we getting somewhere? Would Padilla tell me if she found out Vander's doctor lied? Or would she merely tell the detectives on the case about the lead?

Dad came in. "You about ready for dinner? I can bring it out here."

"No, I should move a little before I stiffen up." I pushed myself forward on the couch. The couch seemed to pull me back. "I think this spot has extra strong gravity though."

"Did you learn anything?" Dad asked.

"Maybe. I guess we should get everyone together to discuss the matter." I yawned. "But not tonight."

After dinner, I sent a group text asking Dad's coffee group to meet at the house in the morning. Joe said he'd bring muffins. Arnold replied: *Accidentally drank invisible ink. Now I'm in the ER waiting to be seen.*

I groaned, chuckled despite myself, and headed up to bed.

Chapter Nineteen

MY PHONE RANG as I entered the kitchen in the morning. "Vander's alibi fell apart," Padilla said in greeting. "Vander made an appointment that day but skipped it."

"Had no one checked with the doctor?" I propped my cane against the counter so I had one hand for the phone and one to get a mug from the cupboard.

"They did, and the doctor confirmed the appointment. The doctor claims it's an honest mistake on his part—he didn't remember, so he trusted the appointment book, which hadn't been updated to no-show."

"Do you believe that?"

I could almost hear her shrug through the phone. "It could be true. Doctors are busy."

"Uh-huh." I eyed the fridge door. My bad leg was throbbing from the unusual exercise the day before, and I was afraid if I tried to get creamer without using one hand to support myself, I'd take a nosedive into the vegetable drawer.

"Or the doctor might've taken a bribe to say Vander had been in his office. Then once he found out it was a murder investigation, he refused to supply an alibi."

"Good to know he has *some* standards," I said. "Was this

the same doctor who prescribed the sedatives to Pamela?"

I could tolerate coffee without creamer for once. I put the phone on speaker and set it on the table so I had both hands free, one for the coffee mug and one to hold on to the back of a chair while I moved the mug from the counter to the table.

"It was. Who knows what she told him to get them? Any excuse would do. Now we know Vander had opportunity, and means wasn't a problem. Motive is still an issue." Padilla paused to answer a question from someone on her end.

I slid into a chair. I stretched and bent my bad leg, sliding my heel along the floor, trying to ease the stiffness. At the same time, I blew on the coffee to cool it down. I never got a jolt from caffeine, but I still craved the ritual of coffee in the morning. I took a cautious sip. Ow, too hot!

Padilla came back on. "The detectives told Vander he'd been seen at the Hodges' house that afternoon. He didn't break."

"Wait a minute, is that true? Was he seen?"

"Unfortunately, no. We did find a camera that caught footage of someone going onto the golf course between a couple of houses on the other side of the grassy part—what's that called, the fairway or something?—from the Hodge house, but it's too far away to identify the person. Don't believe those shows where they can zoom in on video footage and get a clear picture."

I struggled to keep up. It was hard to concentrate on her words when my tongue burned. "So you can't prove he was there, but you said you could, and he kept denying it."

"Right. Most of the time, if the suspect really was there,

they'll start to backtrack, make excuses. That's how we catch them. You get them to admit they were at the scene, and that they lied about it. They come up with new excuses to explain their presence and get tangled in their own lies. But Vander clammed up. Said they could arrest him, and he'd call a lawyer, or he was walking out. They don't have enough to arrest him yet."

"Do you think his reaction indicates innocence or guilt?" I asked.

"Impossible to say. Career criminals are the hardest to break, because they know how the law works. Some of them are sharper than their own lawyers."

"Are you saying Vander is a career criminal?"

Muffled voices came from the background. Then silence. I checked to see if the call had disconnected. Padilla must have muted me. Had she even heard my question?

"He had a shoplifting arrest as a teenager," she said when she came back on. "One drug arrest that wasn't enough to get him charged with intent to sell, but I know the officer who arrested him." Her voice dropped to a whisper. "I wouldn't be surprised if some drugs disappeared before they were checked in, but you didn't hear that from me. Nothing in the last few years, but that could merely mean he's gotten better about not getting caught."

"Dad's friends say Vander is a layabout who doesn't have a job. Of course, that could partly be 'get off my lawn' resentment of the younger generation."

"He's done mainly short-term and seasonal work," Padilla said. "He listed his current employment as a bartender at Cocktail-Palooza. That's a trendy place. Good tips might explain his spending habits. He wouldn't be the only bartender to forget about some of his tip income at tax time. Or he could have an alternative source of income that the police haven't found yet."

"Okay, thanks for—"

She cut me off. "Gotta go."

I got the creamer, doctored my coffee, and left the creamer on the table so I wouldn't have to keep getting in and out of the fridge. While I waited for everyone to arrive, I updated my notes and tried to find patterns. I could ignore the doorbell, knowing Dad and Jen were on that job.

Everyone had the means. Almost anyone might have had the opportunity. It came down to motive. How to make a motive fit the facts?

Clarence and Arnold arrived together. They helped themselves to coffee and sat down.

"Cream?" I pushed the carton toward them.

"No thanks," Clarence said. "I like coffee that reminds me of my ex-wife. Strong and bitter."

"Cute," I said.

"What do you call a coffee joke?" Arnold asked. "A brewhaha."

"I got a million of them," Clarence said. "My ex told me they were grounds for divorce."

It was a good thing these guys had found each other. They were amusing for a few minutes a day, but that was all the *pun*ishment I could take.

Joe and Marty brought mocha chocolate chip banana muffins Joe had made. Larry wasn't invited—we wouldn't be able to discuss the suspects openly with him present.

After coffee and muffins, and Arnold and Clarence telling jokes that were usually bad and often raunchy, we got down to business.

I explained what I'd learned from Detective Padilla.

"It has to be Vander," Joe said.

"I wouldn't go that far," I said. "I agree he's our main suspect now. But we don't know his motive, and we can't prove he did it."

"I can see him killing both Larry and Pamela," Marty said. "Even if they died at the same time, Vander and Vanna could try to claim half the estate. Why only kill his mother? He doesn't gain."

"Do we need to know why?" Clarence asked. "If he did it, he did it!"

"You may not need to know, but a jury might," Dad said.

"Larry and Vanna might too," Marty said.

I tapped my pen on my notepad. "I've been trying to recreate what happened that day. We removed Larry from the house. No one knew we were going to do that. We don't know if Pamela discovered his absence. Given her general level of care for Larry, she might have ignored him as long as he was quiet. He got back to the house around the time of the murder—could be earlier, could be later."

"I don't like the idea that you and Larry might have been there with her dead, or dying," Dad said. "That's disturbing."

"I don't like it either. If she was injured but not dead yet, I might have been able to help her."

Arnold scowled. "I'm glad I didn't have that choice. It

would be too tempting to let her die."

"You wouldn't do that," Clarence said.

"I suppose not. Still, I wish Kate had found her there, dead, when she took Larry back. Then they couldn't suspect Larry. Too late now. I suppose I could claim I went in . . ."

"And get yourself arrested?" Clarence asked. "How would you explain not reporting finding Pamela dead?"

Arnold nodded and slumped back, his gaze on the paper napkin he was shredding.

"As I was saying." I spoke louder than necessary, but I got everyone's attention. "Let's say someone came in and hit Pamela. No, let's go ahead and say *Vander* came in and hit Pamela. He didn't hit her that hard, but she fell and hit her head. Maybe he looked for Larry next. Maybe he would have killed Larry, but Larry wasn't back yet. Either Vander left then, or he left when he heard me come back with Larry."

They were silent for a minute. "You're suggesting Vander meant to kill both of them," Marty said.

"Or he only meant to kill Larry," I said. "Killing his mother was an accident. He wanted to hit her hard enough to leave a bruise. Then she could claim a home invader killed Larry."

The silence lasted longer.

"It explains everything." Dad's shoulders hunched forward. He wrapped both hands around his coffee mug. "Pamela would inherit everything. Vander would take his share. This means Pamela and Vander were in this together."

"Do you believe she could have done something like that?" I asked.

Dad nodded, looking sad.

"From what we know of her," Joe said.

"She was willing to sedate her husband and put him in a home for dementia patients," Marty said. "Killing her husband isn't much of a step from there."

Arnold's chair screeched as he pushed it back and stood. "I hate her! She deserved to die."

Clarence patted his arm. "I know. It's okay. Karma got her."

Arnold sank down again. "But it didn't get Vander. Not yet."

"That's why we have to," Dad said. "We have to trap him somehow."

I winced. I hated to admit he had a point.

I could give my reasoning to Padilla, or even to Detectives Olabarria and Quarterman, and let them try to prove what happened. But Vander had already shown he was smart enough to keep quiet when the police leaned on him. What if they never proved he did it? We'd never know for sure.

Vander no longer had a reason to kill Larry, but he could pursue his wrongful death suit. Even if Vander lost, it would likely cost Larry money and cause stress in the last years of his life. If no one was arrested for Pamela's murder, some people might still suspect Larry killed his wife. That wasn't fair to Larry.

"What about Vanna?" Marty asked. "Was she in on it?"

All eyes turned toward me, as if I were now the expert on psychology, family relationships, and what had happened without our knowledge.

"I'm going to say no." I was guessing, but it was an informed guess. "Her reactions, her behavior, fit with someone taken by surprise. Pamela and Vander didn't need Vanna's help. She wasn't there for the actual murder, and they'd set it up for Larry's children to discover the scene. Vanna happened to get there first, only because Wendy got the time wrong."

"Poor Vanna," Marty murmured. "Now she'll learn her brother killed their mother."

"How do we prove it?" Arnold asked.

Dad turned toward me. "You said the police told him someone saw him in the neighborhood."

I nodded, not liking where this was going.

"That's me," Dad said. "I'm the only one who has admitted to being in the neighborhood, so it would make sense that I'm the one who saw him. I'll tell him I saw him and see what he does."

"Do you think he'll admit his crime to you?" Marty asked.

"He might," Dad said. "We can record the conversation in case he does. If nothing else, it might cause him to do something foolish."

"Like attack you? We can't let that happen." Since Joe voiced that opinion, I didn't have to.

Dad spread his hands. "What do you suggest? We have to get him to reveal himself somehow."

People talked over each other, full of opinions and alternate suggestions. I didn't hear anything that made more sense.

When the chatter died down, I said, "You can try calling Vander. We'll record the conversation. It's even legal as long as you approve the recording."

"What's Isaac going to say?" Marty asked. "He saw Vander and he's calling to tell him so? Isn't that a little obvious that it's a setup?"

"I've been thinking about that," Dad said. "What if I ask for money to keep quiet?"

We all studied Dad. He seemed an unlikely blackmailer.

"Then why would you tell the police about seeing him in the first place?" Marty asked.

"Maybe I didn't get the idea right away," Dad said.

"So you're a lousy blackmailer?" Joe chuckled. "That's easier to believe than seeing you as some kind of villain."

"If Vander was willing to kill an old man for money, he doesn't have much respect for humanity," Dad said. "He'll be willing to believe other people are equally terrible."

"He probably doesn't have any money to pay a blackmailer," Clarence said.

"Who cares?" Arnold said. "We're not actually trying to get money."

I sipped my coffee and waited for the chatter to die down again. It gave me time to consider the problems.

When I thought I'd be heard, I told Dad, "Even if you had seen Vander, that wouldn't prove he murdered Pamela. You can play it like you know he might get off anyway, but you'll make his life easier if he makes Larry's life easier by dropping the wrongful death suit."

"So I'm not believable as a blackmailer, but it's believable that I'd let a murderer go free?" Dad asked.

"You should let me do it," Arnold said. "I've taken acting classes."

"Stand-up comedy isn't acting," Clarence said. "Anyway,

they're talking about a phone call."

"It's harder to lie with only your voice," Arnold said.

What a joy it was having so many assistants to make things easier.

"Dad makes more sense as the person who saw Vander," I said. Besides, I trusted him more not to go off half-cocked and make things worse. I turned my attention to Dad. "Remember, you don't have to convince him that your behavior is logical. You want to scare him. Best case scenario, he admits something that can be used in court."

"And if he doesn't?" Dad asked.

"We know he's willing to kill." I tried to suppress the chill I felt. "If we poke the tiger, we have to assume it might attack. That means following him, knowing exactly where he is and what he's doing at all times."

"We catch him in the act of threatening to hurt me," Dad said.

"Don't look so happy about it," I grumbled. "We'd prefer not to catch him in the act of killing you. But maybe he'll do something to try to cover his tracks. I wish we could convince him there's a piece of evidence he needs to retrieve, something that doesn't involve confronting you directly."

"Larry's house is still empty," Clarence said. "Something there? Evidence Vander left behind?"

"We'd have to convince him the police missed whatever it was," I said.

"What about an outdoor camera?" Arnold bounced in his seat. "We can say Larry installed one in the back, or maybe a neighbor has one trained on the house, and the police don't know about this camera. Wait, we don't want to put someone else in danger, so no neighbors."

We discussed that for a minute. Why wouldn't the police know about the camera? Would Vander have to get the camera itself, or the recordings, which would be on a computer? How could we set that up?

"I hate to say it, but Dad is the bait," I finally said. "There's nothing that works better."

"So I call him." Dad lifted his phone.

I grabbed his arm. "Not until we know where Vander is right now and have people in place to watch him."

Arnold looked at Clarence. "We can take the first shift."

"Okay," I said. "Go to his apartment. We need to know absolutely for certain where he is at all times. Ring the bell to see if he's there." I wrinkled my nose. "Vander will remember Arnold better after their fight at the funeral home. Maybe he didn't notice Clarence." I was starting to understand that many people didn't pay much attention to the elderly, and to someone Vander's age, that might mean anyone over fifty.

"I'll put on a suit and pretend I'm peddling religion," Clarence said. "Bet you he slams the door so fast he doesn't get a good look at me."

My phone buzzed with a group text from Mackenzie to Jen and me: *Eric and developer meeting today!!! Nice public park. Join them? 1 p.m.*

It was after ten. That didn't give us much time to plan a sting operation.

"Okay," I told the group. "You all figure out how you're going to keep Vander under surveillance. Once you find him, Dad can call. Keep me posted."

I drank the last of my coffee and pushed back my chair. Jen closed her notebook and stood.

"Where are you two going?" Dad asked.

"We have an errand to run. Don't set up any meetings until this evening at the earliest."

By that time, we should be finished with Eric Konietzko and Zane Dale, at least for the day.

Chapter Twenty

JEN AND I met Mackenzie at the park. The playground was way fancier than anything Jen and I had growing up. It had swings, complicated jungle gyms, towers with slides, and even a small climbing wall, everything made of brightly colored plastic. We walked on material that felt slightly spongy, which probably did a nice job of cushioning falls but threw off my balance.

"I feel ridiculous," I grumbled, tugging on the elastic waistband of my floral skirt. I literally couldn't remember the last time I'd worn a dress or skirt, and I wouldn't have chosen a floral print then.

"We both look ridiculous," Jen said. "That's the goal."

We'd dug through Mom's closet to find clothes she hadn't worn since the eighties. The calf-length dresses and skirts in pastel colors might have been fashionable in certain circles then. They might even look fashionable now, on someone they fit properly. With my mismatched top and too-long skirt, and the pink sweater with pearl buttons Jen wore over a green and blue dress, plus our sneakers, straw hats from the hall closet, and my cane, we looked ready to star in a movie about old broads who'd escaped from a nursing home to hit Vegas with their social security money.

I had to admit, it was the perfect disguise to ensure a thirtysomething man wouldn't notice our faces and would avoid even looking in our direction after the first glance.

Mackenzie wore a ball cap and sunglasses, with her blond hair in a high ponytail. She also wore a low-cut tank top and very short shorts. That was another way to inspire a thirtysomething man going through a divorce to not notice a woman's face. She had been lurking in the background at the climbing gym, and Eric had been plenty distracted, but we weren't taking chances.

"Eric is waiting on the bench over there." Mackenzie jerked her chin to point across the playground.

He sat hunched forward on the bench, apparently focused on his phone.

The playground wasn't crowded on a Friday at one, but over a dozen kids ran around the place. Almost as many adults chatted with each other or studied their electronic devices. A couple of people stretched out on the plastic benches, dozing in the winter sun.

"I can see why they chose this spot," Jen said. "With all the kids running around, it's hard to tell if an adult is with one of them or alone. People might view a single man with suspicion, but he isn't paying attention to the kids. He could be a neglectful dad, a businessman getting some sun, or a dude hoping to hit on hot moms. Or all three, I suppose. Most people will stay away from him."

"Unfortunately, we need to get a lot closer if we're going to overhear anything," I said. "But if we get too close, we might attract his attention. Even if he doesn't recognize us and we look harmless, these guys might be cautious about saying anything suspicious with witnesses nearby."

"Right." Jen frowned. "If we make them nervous, they'll move. We can't follow Eric and Zane Dale all over the playground."

"Like a slow-motion game of tag," I said.

"We need a recording device." Jen clapped her hands together. "I read about these ones that look like pens. You could drop one behind his bench and retrieve it later. I might order one, for the future."

She thought we'd be doing this a lot?

Maybe she was right. I hadn't predicted doing it the first time, so what did I know?

"We have recording devices." Mackenzie held up her phone.

"Dropping a phone behind them might be a little obvious," Jen said.

"I have an idea. Be right back." Mackenzie jogged toward the parking lot.

Jen and I found a bench about thirty feet from Eric. Jen took a few photos. "I think we're close enough to zoom in and see them clearly."

We could get photos of city council member Eric Konietzko and housing developer Zane Dale, to prove they'd met here. But meeting wasn't illegal. It might be odd that they met at a playground instead of an office, but they could make excuses for that easily enough. We needed to know what they said, and ideally record it. The recording wouldn't be legal in court, since we didn't have the permission of anyone in the conversation, but Todd could use it to get Eric to back down.

My phone rang. "It's Mackenzie," I answered. "Hello?"

"Put yourself on mute," she said.

I did. "Okay." Of course now she couldn't hear me.

Mackenzie headed for Eric at a leisurely stroll, ignoring us. She carried a thin cord a couple of feet long. She passed behind his bench and then leaned over it with a hand to his shoulder. Her voice came through the phone, though it sounded lower pitched than usual. "Mind if I plug in here? The benches by the sandbox aren't working."

"Oh. Sure." Eric's voice also came through the phone.

"Great. Thanks so much."

"What's she doing?" I squinted, trying to make out the details.

"She's plugging her phone into the charging dock on the bench," Jen said.

I turned to stare at my sister. "They have charging docks in the playground?"

"Sure." Jen waved a hand around. "Look at all these women on their laptops or phones while the kids play. Gotta have someplace to plug in."

I was still grateful when an airport had free charging stations and I didn't have to fight over the one or two outlets in a waiting area that seated dozens. Would I ever stop getting that jolt when I realized people in the US took for granted something I didn't know existed?

"Are you going to be here awhile?" Mackenzie asked. "You look trustworthy, but I wouldn't want my phone lying around unattended."

"I'll probably be here for fifteen minutes or so."

"That might be enough to boost my battery." The way

Mackenzie said it almost sounded dirty. "I'll put my ball cap over my phone to hide it. If you have to leave, don't worry. I won't be far, and I'll keep an eye on you from over there."

Eric watched as Mackenzie strolled away, hips swaying. She went to a circular sandbox for little kids and sat on one of the benches there. She could easily pass for a babysitter, nanny, or young mother. Either Eric was so distracted by her looks that he didn't consider the possibility of her phone as a spy device, or he was so used to phones and chargers everywhere that he didn't think anything of it. Either way, good for us.

Eric looked up as a man in a sports jacket approached. The new guy looked older, maybe in his fifties, with short salt-and-pepper hair and broad shoulders. He sank to the bench and scanned the area, not looking at Eric.

"That's Zane Dale," Jen whispered. "I saw his picture online."

"Thanks for coming," Eric said.

"What's so urgent?" Zane Dale asked.

I turned on a recording app. Mackenzie might have done the same on her phone, but it wouldn't hurt to have backup. Jen and I hunched over my phone, trying to hear. The voices were faint, but we could make out most of the words.

"My wife." Eric used a few unflattering terms for Carly. "She's threatening to have me audited for the divorce."

Zane Dale laughed. "Sucks to be you."

Jen's breath whispered past my ear. "Forgot to tell you: Carly said she did that this morning. I figured it couldn't hurt and might light a fire under Eric—which it did."

"Are you sure no one can track your payments to my accounts?" Eric asked.

"Not if you set them up properly. You made a shell corporation, right? Don't pay yourself from that company until the divorce is final."

"Yeah, but I'm an officer in that company. A good lawyer will find it."

"Get yourself a better lawyer," Zane Dale said. "Your wife has her own store, right? She tries to get part of your company, you demand part of hers. She'll back down."

"Okay. Right. I'm sure it's fine."

We could hear Eric's breathing through the phone, suggesting he wasn't quite as calm as he pretended.

"Is that it?" Dale asked.

Eric shifted on the bench. "The thing is . . ." His voice dropped and I couldn't catch what he said next.

Dale laughed again. "Getting greedy?"

"You're one to talk," Eric grumbled. "I've seen your mansion. It's this divorce. I'm losing a lot of communal property. If I'm going to run for mayor, I need to present the right front. I need a house where I can entertain. The right clothes, a nice car."

"Not too nice," Dale said. "People get suspicious of politicians who drive Ferraris."

"Yeah, but they trust guys who drive BMWs," Eric said. "They trust nice suits. They may pretend they want a man of the people, but ordinary folks look up to successful men. You need to be what they want to be. Act successful to create success, right?"

"Let's get the current deal through," Dale said. "Show me you can do that. I'll look around at other properties that might be worth developing. You'll have to get me really good perks though."

Eric nodded, but whatever he said didn't come through to us. Drat. Well, maybe the recording picked it up better. Otherwise, we wouldn't be able to prove that Eric had agreed to Zane Dale's terms.

The developer stood. He said something without looking down at Eric, so only a couple of words filtered through. Something about pleasure and business.

Eric sat for another minute before he rose and headed toward Mackenzie. We couldn't hear what he said to her, but she ran across to retrieve her phone and hat. She headed into the women's restroom. That was a good way to make sure Eric didn't try to get friendly.

Mackenzie's voice came through my phone louder, and I jumped.

"Let me know when he's gone."

"Right." I stopped the recording on my phone. Eric dawdled another minute. He glanced our way and his gaze slid right past Jen and me. He finally headed to the parking lot. I told Mackenzie she could come out.

Mackenzie joined us and dropped to the peach-colored foam outdoor flooring, sitting cross-legged. "How did it go?"

"You were brilliant," I said. "I don't know if what we got could convict either of them of crimes, but this recording sure makes them look bad."

"Now what?" Jen asked.

"I'll give the recording to Todd. It might be enough to spike the current deal, if Todd shares it with the rest of the city council or threatens to do so if Eric doesn't change his vote. It might even keep Eric from running for mayor or provide ammo against him if he does. He might not be wrong about people trusting nice suits, but no one wants to hear that about themselves."

"So we're done?" Jen sounded so disappointed.

"At least for now," I said. "Congratulations on your first investigation. You helped topple the government, or at least root out jerks at the local level."

"I'll send you my recording of the file," Mackenzie said. "I'm gonna be late if I don't run."

"Go."

She literally ran for the parking lot. Jen and I watched her. I don't know what Jen was thinking, but I couldn't help pining for the days when my legs had been that young and strong.

A child ran past with a shriek that made my eardrums throb. A woman yelled at the child, who completely ignored every command.

Jen heaved a sigh. "I miss those days."

"The days of chasing after bratty children?"

"Don't knock it till you've tried it," she said.

"No thanks. I have enough trouble keeping my parents in line."

Jen sat up straighter and the sparkle came back to her eyes. "That's right. We still get to catch Vander."

"I'll give Dad a call and see if there's any progress."

I hung up a minute later. "Good news, from a certain perspective. Vander is working at Cocktail-Palooza tonight and asked Dad to come by and talk to him there at nine. That sounds like he's taking the bait. Problem is, it's going to be loud in a cocktail bar, making it hard to get a decent recording, and we don't want Dad going off someplace secluded with Vander. I guess we'll go and see what happens. If we're all on alert, we can stop him doing anything to hurt Dad." I hoped.

Jen's brows drew together. "Cocktail-Palooza. Where else have I heard that name?" She pulled out her phone and tapped at it. "Oh, right. They have a cocktail-making class every Friday at six! I was thinking we should try it."

"Today happens to be Friday." I pondered. "The class might give us a chance to scope out the place. We can stay after for Dad's meeting."

"Hey, big sister." She nudged my shoulder. "Want to hit up a bar tonight?"

"I guess cocktail making beats rock climbing, at least when it comes to physical difficulty." I gestured at our outfits. "We might want a different disguise though."

Jen's eyes gleamed. "I know just the thing."

I whimpered. What had I gotten myself into now?

Chapter Twenty-One

WE DEBATED WHETHER we needed disguises at all. We wanted Vander to panic enough to do something to reveal himself. Would it help if he knew we were keeping an eye on him?

But if he got *too* nervous, he might freeze up or go into hiding. We knew he wasn't afraid to confront one old man, so we'd let him think that was all he had to face. If he knew we were watching him, he might change his plans, putting Dad in more danger.

So, more disguises. Jen hadn't met Vander, so she was fine. I'd had a lengthy face-to-face conversation with Vander. My disguise had to be good.

The "old lady" disguise had discouraged Eric from looking at me closely. That wouldn't be enough for a two-hour class at a bar where Vander was working. My face had to look different.

It's easier to look older than you really are, but a cocktail-making class at a trendy bar would probably be filled with people in their twenties and thirties. We decided to attempt to look younger, or at least somewhat youthful and hip, although *hip* probably wasn't the word today's stylish young people would use.

Jen brought me a short black skirt belonging to her teenage daughter, along with a pair of black leggings to hide my scars. Then she went to work on my makeup. I don't know if I achieved stylish, but the look knocked a few years off, and if I hardly recognized myself in the mirror, maybe Vander wouldn't notice me in a crowd. Jen's daughter also had temporary hair dye, so I tinted my silver with purple.

The cane and the limp were still problematic as distinguishing features. I didn't want anything to catch Vander's attention and clue him in to why I seemed familiar.

Good thing Mayor Todd Paradise owed me a favor.

He had a friend with an SUV who would pick us up and drop us off in front of the bar, so I wouldn't have to walk far. Jen, Todd, and I would take over surveillance, so Clarence and Arnold could get dinner. We'd stick around after the cocktail class, pretending to be regular bar patrons. At nine o'clock, Arnold and Clarence would wait out back behind the bar, while Joe and Marty stayed in their car, ready to follow if Vander somehow got Dad into a vehicle. When Dad met Vander, he'd have a whole team as backup.

Todd arrived with a bouquet of flowers. The word *chrysanthemum* popped into my head from somewhere, but don't quote me on that. I could tell an AK-47 from an AK-74, but I might struggle to differentiate between a chrysanthemum and a carnation.

I stared at the bouquet for a second. "Thanks." Was this a romantic gesture? Gratitude for dealing with his city council problem?

I mentally shrugged, went to the kitchen to put them in a vase with water, and hoped Jen wouldn't say anything to embarrass me in my absence but didn't count on it. I put the vase on the little table inside our front door, among the keys and mail, and we headed out.

During the drive, I messaged Clarence. He confirmed Vander was still at the bar. Everything seemed to be going as planned.

Getting out of an SUV had never bothered me before, but I hadn't tried it since I'd hurt my leg—or while wearing a short skirt. I hesitated with the back door open, eyeing the ground, which seemed ridiculously far away.

Todd stood in front of me. "Need a hand?"

He offered me two of them, holding my waist and lifting me down. I touched the ground and wobbled in my heels, which were only two inches high, but that was two inches higher than normal for me. I grabbed Todd's upper arms for balance.

He smelled great, like an ocean breeze.

"You do this often?" Todd asked.

"Go to bars? Dress like this? Spy on a possible murderer? No. Well, maybe the last one, but usually not at a hot nightspot."

He chuckled. "I thought you might use disguises for your investigative reporting."

"Not really. In Arab countries, I might wear an abaya or burka, whatever the local version is of the loose robe women wear, but that's more about fitting in and respecting the local culture. And not getting harassed in the street for showing too much forearm or ankle."

"I guess men are the same everywhere."

"Well, when the men doing the harassing are religious

police berating you for improper dress, I suppose the motive is different."

I looked past Todd's shoulder. Jen waited a few feet away, smirking. She caught my gaze and made kissing motions.

Sisters. I resisted the urge to make a face back at her. I did, however, express my feelings with a subtle hand gesture as I released Todd's arms.

He turned, offering an elbow out. I tucked my hand through it. Jen crossed to my other side. I thought I could manage short distances without my cane, but it helped to have someone to lean on. Stumbling and sprawling across a table full of drinks would not keep me under the radar.

We stepped inside. Jen talked to the host, showing our reservation for the class.

The host led us to a table. The people gathered for the cocktail-making class had a wider variety of ages than I'd expected. I was probably only the third oldest person there, with Todd and Jen close behind. Several people appeared to be in their forties. Some of the younger crowd looked ready for clubbing, and one fortyish couple had dressed for date night, but jeans predominated. I was overdressed, but the point wasn't so much to fit in as it was to avoid Vander's recognition, and he'd seen me in shorts and T-shirt before.

I still felt weird. I liked to think I could adapt to most situations and fit in most places, but this was outside my comfort zone. Like, a continent away from my comfort zone.

In the dim lighting, it took me a minute to identify Vander as one of the three people behind the bar. He mainly looked down at whatever he was doing, but occasionally he flashed glances around the dimly lit room. I didn't debate whether he had the face of a murderer. I'd learned that you couldn't tell who might kill, or under what circumstances, by looking at people. I did wonder what he was thinking now. Was he planning what he would say and do when Dad arrived later? Did he already have a plan? Would he try to talk his way out of Dad's accusations, or would he try to get rid of a loose end?

The class started, and for a while I was distracted. The host explained the various items used to make cocktails, like shakers and stirrers. Then the staff brought shot glasses with different liquors and add-ons, so we could smell the various options and try to identify the flavor elements.

"I thought the smell thing was only for wine," Jen whispered.

I sniffed the shot glass holding a splash of whiskey and wrinkled my nose. "I'm going to say . . . woody? Kind of like fresh-cut pine sawdust though, not like aged oak." I took another sniff. "And something sharp and acidic."

"Band-Aids," Todd said.

"That's it." Jen made a note in the booklet they'd given each of us. "I was going to say hand sanitizer, but it's Band-Aids."

"Trust the parents to know those smells." I made a note in my own booklet. "Why would anyone want to drink Band-Aids?"

Todd gave me a haughty look. "Clearly you don't understand sophisticated tastes."

I snorted, which definitely showed my level of sophistication. That sent us all into a fit of laughter.

The host came over.

"Sorry," Jen said.

"You're fine," the man said. "This is supposed to be fun. Any questions?"

We chatted for a couple of minutes before he moved on to the next table.

I doodled in the booklet and glanced around the bar. The bartenders worked the room, answering questions, bringing clean glasses, or making full-size cocktails on request. The room had gotten louder and drunker.

Someone was missing.

"Where's Vander?"

Jen had the shot glass to her lips, her head tipped back. She choked on the alcohol and coughed as she looked around. "What?"

We scanned the bar. No sign of him.

"He could be in back getting more supplies," I said, "or in the bathroom. Todd, can you check the men's restroom?"

He headed for a back hallway.

Jen and I exchanged worried looks.

"He was here a few minutes ago," Jen said.

"How long since you last saw him?"

We discussed it and realized it had been as long as ten minutes since we'd seen him for certain.

Todd came back and leaned over the table between us. "He's not in the restroom, and I took a peek in the storeroom. No one's there. The end of the hallway has a door leading out the back to a small parking lot. I didn't see anyone outside."

I felt light-headed, and it certainly wasn't from the minute amount of alcohol I'd consumed. I pushed to my feet. Todd grabbed my arm to steady me.

"We have to go," I said.

We hurried out with a quick excuse to the host.

Todd looked up and down the street. "Shoot, my friend wasn't going to pick us up for another two hours."

"I'll call a car service." Jen pulled out her phone.

Cars passed by, and a few pedestrians headed into the restaurants and bars on the block.

"Great. A car is within one minute," Jen said. "That's the advantage of Friday night in the party district. Where are we going? We can't follow him if we can't see him and don't know where he went."

"I'm trying to think." I held on to Todd's arm, partly for balance and partly to keep myself grounded in this time and place. My gut said it was time to panic. My mind hadn't quite caught up to why, let alone the proper response.

"Okay," I said. "Vander asked Dad to meet him here at nine. That made sense, because it was after the cocktail class but before the bar would get too busy. What time is it now?"

Jen glanced at her phone. "Almost eight."

"So your guy could be coming back for the meeting," Todd said.

"Maybe, but we half expected him to do something drastic. We *wanted* him to do something drastic. Meeting his blackmailer in a public place isn't. We thought maybe he'd try to get Dad to leave with him, go someplace more secluded."

"And we'd stop him before he could hurt Dad," Jen said.

I nodded. "But what if the whole meeting was a ruse?

What if Vander suspected Dad might have backup at a meeting? He scheduled the meeting so we'd let down our guard."

A car pulled up. "That's ours," Jen said.

We scrambled into the back seat, first Jen, then me, then Todd.

Jen looked at me. "Where are we going?"

"Home. Give him the address. I'll call Dad."

Dad's phone rang.

Answer, answer. Maybe I was wrong. Maybe Vander had stepped out for a smoke, and Todd hadn't seen him around the side of the building. Maybe the bar sent him for supplies. That one table was really going through the tequila. The bar might have run out.

Dad's phone rang and rang. He should be home. He should be answering.

His voice mail picked up. I left a message. "Dad, watch out. We think he might be coming for you now. Call me back when you get this. Be safe."

I sank back in the seat, cold and trembling.

"We'll be there in eight minutes," Jen said.

Todd took my free hand, the one that wasn't still gripping my phone. "Hang in there. It will be all right."

I clung to his hand. I was not convinced it would be all right, but the warmth of his hand helped.

"Can you explain what you think is happening?" Todd asked.

"I could be wrong," I said. "I hope I am. But what if Vander headed to our house to deal with Dad now? He takes a break, or maybe he just slips out and hopes nobody will notice how long he's gone. He gets rid of the witness to his earlier murder—makes it look like another break-in."

I couldn't continue.

"Shouldn't we call the police?" Todd asked.

Of course we should. Even if I was wrong, it was better to look foolish than risk Dad.

I stared at my phone. Should I try to reach Detective Padilla, who knew me and the situation? But 911 would provide the fastest response.

"I don't know how to explain all this to them," I said.

"Leave that to me." He pulled out his phone. "You keep thinking."

As if I could stop. My mind kept racing through the possibilities. "Tell them to keep quiet. If Vander hears sirens outside, we might wind up with a hostage situation."

Jen and I clasped hands. None of this felt real—my outfit, a stranger's car, Todd beside me dressed as if for a date, Dad waiting at home, planning for a meeting that would never happen.

I'd assumed we were smarter than Vander, that we could play him.

If I was wrong, Dad was the one who would suffer.

Chapter Twenty-Two

WE HAD THE driver stop a few houses down from Dad's, so we wouldn't alert anyone in the house. We scrambled out. Todd was still on the phone. He pointed toward a police car parked down the street as the officer got out.

"Please explain the situation to them," I said.

He nodded and headed that way. Gotta appreciate a man who can follow instructions.

Jen and I stared at the house. It seemed quiet enough, with a few lights on downstairs and Jen's car parked in the driveway. I didn't see the car Vander and Vanna had at the funeral home, but an unfamiliar motorcycle stood across the street and down a few houses.

"Now what?" Jen said. "We let the police do their thing?"

I looked at my phone, as if it might magically ring because I wanted it to do so. It stayed silent. Why hadn't Dad answered or called back?

Was he already dead?

I shoved that thought out of my head, but I couldn't suppress the shiver that ran through my body.

"I want to get in there," I said. "We don't know how

much time we have."

He might be injured, bleeding, as Pamela had lain bleeding, slowly dying even as I snuck Larry back into the house.

"If he came after Dad to hide his crimes, he won't hesitate to hurt us too," Jen said.

"I've had self-defense training. I used to practice with one of the bodyguards."

"Used to, you mean before—" She gestured at my leg.

"Yeah, but it's not about strength. It's about knowing how to do the most damage quickly. You go for the eyes, throat, crotch. Drop to the ground and kick their knees." I could do that with one good leg.

"How does that work against a gun?"

I swallowed. "Vander hasn't used a gun." Hopefully he didn't have one.

I started toward the house. Jen grabbed my arm. I wobbled in my heels. I wanted to wrench my arm out of her grip, but at the moment she was helping me stay upright. My cane was in the house, since I hadn't planned on being without human support.

"I'm worried about Dad too," Jen hissed, "but I don't want to lose both of you. I don't care what fancy moves you know. This guy is dangerous."

"I know that." I moved forward, dragging her along. "He doesn't know I can be dangerous. That gives me the advantage. In fact—unlock your car."

"Why?" She pulled out her keys and hit the button. The car beeped, and we both winced. I hurried to the car's back door, keeping an eye on the house. With the shades drawn, we'd be able to see if anyone moved them to look out.

I opened the car door, and the inside light went on. I grabbed our costumes from that afternoon and quickly closed the door again. Still no one at the windows. I tossed the bundle of costumes on the trunk.

"What are you doing?" Jen asked.

"Looking harmless." I pulled the loose floral skirt up over my short black skirt and slipped into the pink sweater Jen had worn. Then I smashed a straw hat on my head. I probably looked ridiculous with the black leggings showing at the bottom of the skirt, but I only had to throw off Vander for a few seconds.

"You think that will keep Vander from trying to hurt you?" Jen asked.

"No, I think it will convince him I'm harmless long enough for me to figure out what's going on."

My tennis shoes would provide better stability but changing would take time. Besides, heels made good weapons.

"You should let me go in," Jen said.

"Do you have to argue with everything I say?"

"Am I your sister?" One corner of her mouth quirked up in a quick smile. "I should go in because I can run. Once I see what's happening, I'll get out of there fast."

It wasn't a criticism or a dig. She meant well. She might even have a point. It was almost always better to run than fight, if you had the choice. But I didn't want to put her in danger either.

"Add martial arts to your list of new hobbies." I squared my shoulders.

"Wait! The makeup doesn't go with your look." Jen

pulled something out of her purse. She scrubbed at my face with a damp wipe. "There. You look awful."

"Thanks." I headed for the house.

My arms and legs tingled. That was good—adrenaline was getting me ready for action, helping me ignore the weakness in one leg. Good, as long as I didn't freeze up or get clumsy.

I tried the door. Locked. We'd taken to locking it since our last problem with being targets of a killer. We really needed to stop doing this.

If Vander was inside, he hadn't gotten in that way. He probably went through the back or a window.

Was that faint thudding sound coming from inside the house?

I had my keys in a little embroidered purse slung across my body on a long strap. The purse was now under my second skirt. I yanked out the purse and fumbled with stiff fingers.

Hissing voices carried to me. I glanced back at the corner of the yard, where Todd and the police officer seemed to be arguing with Jen. No time to lose if I wanted to get inside before they tried to stop me.

I unlocked the door and pushed it open. One step inside, I stopped and glanced around. No one visible in what I could see of the living room to my left. A repetitive banging sound came from the kitchen to the right, but I couldn't see through that archway. It sounded like someone pounding on a door, not knocking but rather trying to break it down.

I went light-headed and swayed. I drew in a deep breath and blinked, trying to clear the spots from my eyes.

My cane leaned against the table that we used for keys, mail, and, at the moment, the vase with Todd's flowers. I grabbed the cane, both for balance and because I'd learned it could be a good defensive weapon if someone rushed you.

I had two choices—move quietly and hope I saw Vander before he saw me, or go in loudly and let the people outside know what I was doing. We hadn't taken the time to set up a hidden phone call or discuss codewords, but I left the door wide open.

"Isaac?" I tried to make my voice a bit high and wavery.

The pounding stopped.

Vander appeared in the archway that led to the kitchen. We stared at each other.

I should say something to put him further off guard.

My mind was blank.

"Who are you?" Vander demanded.

"I live here," I said. "I'm Isaac's wife." That should explain any familiarity about me, while convincing him to dismiss me as a feeble senior.

I was two steps inside, with the door open behind me. A faint rustle suggested someone creeping closer—hopefully the police officer. If Vander came after me, I could dart outside, dive behind a bush, and let the police deal with him.

Well, "dart and dive" might be optimistic, but "stumble and fall" could work.

"What are you doing in my kitchen?" I asked loudly, so the people outside would know his location. "Where's Isaac?"

"He stepped into the bathroom." Vander smiled. "Come on in and have a drink with us."

We eyed each other. I wanted him to come to me, and he wanted me to go to him. I wasn't sure what to make of the pounding I'd heard. My stomach churned at the thought that maybe he'd been beating on Dad. But it had sounded like hitting wood—surely a body wouldn't sound like that, it wouldn't, it wouldn't—so maybe Dad had barricaded himself behind a door. From the kitchen, doors led outside, to the laundry room, and to the basement. If Dad went out back, Vander wouldn't have to break the door down to follow. I didn't think the laundry room door had a lock, but the basement did.

Regardless, I wanted to get Vander out into the open entryway, closer to the outside door and reinforcements.

"It's awfully late for a drink," I said. "I'll head up to bed and leave you to it." That would draw him forward. He wouldn't let me go now that I'd seen him.

Though maybe he'd wait until I took a few steps up the stairs and he could get behind me.

I did not want him behind me.

Something moved in the kitchen behind Vander.

I spoke loudly to cover any noise. "Actually, I think you should go now. It's late and I'm tired and you should get out of here—"

"I can't do that." Vander stepped toward me. "You—I know you." His eyes narrowed. "What's wrong with your face?"

I held my ground, my body taut as a bowstring, staring into Vander's eyes to keep his attention on me. "My face is perfectly fine."

Behind him, something black arced through the air toward his head.

Vander must have heard or sensed something. He started to turn.

The black object smashed into his cheek. Dad stood behind him, holding—was that the coffee grinder?

Vander grunted and stumbled against the archway. He shook his head hard.

I stepped forward and swung my cane at his ankle.

He yelped, yanking that foot upward. I brought the cane back in a circle and whacked his knee.

He slid past the archway and fell against the little table along the entryway wall. Vander sprawled on the floor. Keys and letters cascaded down on him. The vase tipped, splashing water over his head. The vase then rolled off the table. Unfortunately, it rolled sideways, hitting the foyer floor instead of his head.

Vander was down, but not out. He swiped a hand across his face and sat up.

I glanced out the front door. The police officer stood with gun drawn, Todd and Jen peering over his shoulders, wide-eyed.

"Come on!" I yelled.

Vander twisted to kneel. In a second, he'd be up where he could grab Dad or me and have a hostage.

Vulnerable spots: eyes, throat, crotch, sternum, instep. Vander wasn't in a position where I could jam my high heel into his instep, and I didn't want to get close enough for a thumb to the eye.

I thrust up my cane, aiming for his throat. The end of the cane hit right in that little divot at the base of the throat.

Vander made a choking sound and jerked back.

The police officer pushed into the entryway and aimed her gun. "Freeze!"

Arms came around me, holding me steady. I slumped against Todd, my legs weak, and not because of the damaged muscles.

Vander's choking died down.

"Get up and put your hands against the wall," the officer said.

"I wasn't—I didn't—" Vander scowled and coughed a couple of times. "I want a lawyer."

"You'll need one to defend you against the charges of murdering your mother," I said.

"I didn't—that wasn't—" He squeezed his eyes shut. "I never wanted my mother to die."

"But she did. You hit her and left her on the floor while you went looking for Larry. You're lucky he wasn't there. You might be able to plea bargain for manslaughter over your mother's death instead of premeditated murder. But you'll have to tell the police what really happened."

Vander looked from me to the police officer's gun still pointing at him and back to me. "Mom was an accident. I thought she was faking being hurt, like we planned. I didn't realize she'd hit her head. It was an accident."

"That's still manslaughter," I said. "And assault. You punched your own mother in the face."

"She told me to! It was all her idea. The whole thing, from the beginning. Larry's friends were getting suspicious, and she didn't think she could keep drugging him forever. She wanted a way out fast, so she came up with the burglary plan. She roped me into it."

"Why did you steal items after hitting your mother, if Larry wasn't home?"

He looked at me blankly. "Because that was the plan. I realized later I shouldn't have done that part, if I wanted to make Larry look guilty. But it was the plan. Her plan. I didn't want to do it."

"Tell it to the jury. They might even believe you." Did I? Maybe it didn't matter who came up with the plan. Pamela was dead, and we had enough evidence against Vander to get him convicted of something. "My mommy made me do it" wouldn't work as a defense for a man his age.

Jen turned to me with a gleeful grin. She held up her phone. "Got that on video!"

The police officer spoke again, slowly enunciating each word. "Get up, turn around, and put your hands against the wall."

Vander stood and turned to face the wall, his hands spread in front of him.

"Can I cuff him?" Jen asked. "You should keep your gun on him."

The officer hesitated, shrugged, and nodded.

While they took care of Vander, Dad skirted around them and came to me. I threw myself into his arms. Todd was great, but at that moment, nothing beat the feel of my father's hug.

Chapter Twenty-Three

HALF AN HOUR later, the house was jam-packed. The police had taken Vander away, but additional officers were taking statements in the living room. The rest of us waited in the kitchen. Clarence, Arnold, Joe, and Marty had joined us. We caught them up on the evening's activities.

"I can't believe you hit Vander with a coffee grinder," I said.

"I didn't want to attract his attention by opening cupboards or drawers. That didn't leave a lot of options." Dad looked around the kitchen. "Maybe from now on we should keep a nice cast-iron skillet on the stove."

He had a point. We kept the kitchen fairly tidy, so no pans, dishes, or knives sat out. The microwave and toaster oven were too heavy and bulky. The coffee maker was awkwardly shaped, and besides, if we broke it, what would we do for coffee in the morning? The coffee grinder was roughly cylindrical and fairly heavy for its size.

"I guess it made as good a weapon as anything here," I said. "You didn't knock him out, but you gave him something to remember you by."

Dad reached across the corner of the table to put his hand over mine. "I kept him from hurting you. That's what counts."

"Dad." I put my other hand over his and squeezed. I still felt shaky remembering the danger he'd been in. "I'm sorry we messed up. Someone should have stayed with you."

"You can't predict every possibility," Dad said. "Perfection is an impossible goal."

"Still," Jen said, "we'll know better for next time."

I might have whimpered a little.

"In any case, you did save me," Dad said. "I was looking for holiday lights in the basement. I haven't felt like putting them up, what with your mother at Sunshine Haven, and all the other stress. Tonight, I felt hopeful. I heard the phone ringing and realized I'd left it on the kitchen counter. I hurried upstairs but didn't make it in time."

"You have no idea how scared I was when I couldn't reach you," I said.

"Oh, I bet I can imagine what it's like when someone you love may be in danger." His hand tightened on mine. "I got to the top of the stairs as Vander broke through the back door. He was blocking my routes out of the kitchen, so I couldn't think of anything better to do than go back into the basement and lock the door."

The basement door now showed signs of Vander's attack in the splintered wood around the lock. Fortunately, he hadn't brought a weapon. He wore gloves and must have assumed he'd find something here to use on Dad, so the object couldn't be traced back to him. Or else he'd simply planned to use his fists.

"He threw himself against the door a few times and then started kicking it," Dad said. "He was about to break through when you called out. The door almost fell off its hinges when I pushed it open. Good thing it didn't, or I wouldn't have been able to sneak up on him. I kept trying to think of what weapons we might have down there. We gave away all your old sports equipment years ago. Then Mom got on a cleaning kick last year, gave a bunch of stuff to the thrift stores. Not much is left besides books, holiday decorations, and boxes of tax files."

Clarence chuckled. "I know how to use tax files as a weapon, but maybe not in this situation."

Jen had her notebook out. She scribbled something in it. "You need a better security system in this house."

"Hey, we've lived here for almost fifty years with no problems," Dad said. "And then your sister comes home . . ."

Everyone laughed.

I gave a huff. "Right, like I'm the troublemaker. Who got me into this?"

"If you weren't so good at it, people wouldn't ask you for help," Jen said.

Would they keep asking? When I'd investigated suspicious deaths at Sunshine Haven, I was trying to protect my mother. I hadn't entirely managed that, but I did uncover crimes.

Now I had helped a friend of Dad's. In fact, if we hadn't done what we'd done, Larry would be dead now. Granted, kidnapping him at the point we did had been pure luck, but he was alive, Vander would pay for his crimes, and Pamela was a casualty of her own greed.

I could be doing worse things with my life.

The oven timer beeped. Joe opened the oven door and

pulled out a batch of cookies he'd whipped up from ingredients in our pantry. The smell of molasses and ginger filled the room. I was suddenly ravenous.

Arnold tipped his head back and sniffed loudly. "Joe, if you weren't married, I'd propose to you right now."

"Hey, I put a lot of work into him," Marty said. "It's finally paying off now that he's discovered baking as an antidote to stress."

Todd came back from his police interview. "I should get going. If I stay out too late, the kids are going to tease me mercilessly about my hot date."

"I'll walk you out." I rose stiffly, my muscles still not recovered from yesterday's rock climbing, let alone this evening's adrenaline. Todd offered his arm, and I took it. I didn't need his help to go the few feet to the front door—but I enjoyed it.

We paused in the foyer. He glanced into the living room, where the police officers were gathering up their things.

"Thanks for the recording," Todd whispered. "This should keep Eric in check."

"Sorry I couldn't get legal evidence to have them both arrested."

"The recording might not hold up in court, but now that I know I'm right, I can alert a couple of people I know to look out for illegal activities. In the meantime, I might be able to force Eric to resign. I owe you one."

I smiled up at him. "I'd say after tonight, we're even. Thanks for your help."

He shrugged. "I just did what you asked me to do."

"Funny thing. That was exactly what I needed. Let me

know how things go."

He kissed my cheek and left.

I said goodbye to the police officers. We'd have to follow up more over the next few days, but we could sleep tonight knowing Vander was in custody.

I stopped in the restroom and realized why the police officers had given me funny looks. When Jen had wiped down my face, she smeared my fancy going-out makeup. I truly did look awful, but less like an elderly woman and more like La Llorona, the drowned, weeping ghost of Hispanic folklore. And nobody had thought to mention this to me for the last hour?

I washed my face, headed back into the kitchen, and slumped into a chair. Joe topped off my mug of decaf. "I saved a couple of cookies for you. It was like a plague of locusts in here."

"Thanks." The two cookies on my plate appeared to be the only ones remaining from the two dozen Joe had pulled from the oven minutes before. "I guess facing death induces hunger."

"What's my excuse?" Joe asked.

Arnold slapped his hand down on the table. "Frustration because we didn't get to smack that scoundrel around ourselves."

I snickered, picturing Dad and all of his coffee buddies standing around Vander, whacking him with various kitchen implements. I almost choked on a cookie crumb.

"What?" Arnold said. "You don't think I'm tough? I can be tough."

Clarence poked Arnold's shoulder. "Tough as a bag of kittens, that's you."

"Hey, kittens have claws and pointy little teeth."

The two men argued cheerfully. Marty helped Joe fill two more trays with cookie dough.

Dad caught my gaze and smiled. "You did good tonight. I may not like that you put yourself in danger that way, but when I heard your voice . . ."

"You didn't actually think it was Mom, did you?"

"No, I'd recognize you anywhere. I was terrified about you going into danger, but also grateful that you were home, and what you said told me you were on alert."

"All I did was distract him so you could take him down," I said. "Arnold is right—you guys are tough."

"Years of experience. Now my body says it wants to sleep for days, but my mind is still too wired."

I nodded. The feeling was familiar from hundreds of perilous situations. Jen was right about a security system. Even if we didn't draw nasty people to our home again, the extra security would help us feel safe. I didn't mind excitement, but home should be a refuge.

It went against my instincts to tell Jen she was right, but waiting until problems dropped into my lap had drawbacks. If I was going to keep doing these kinds of investigations, I needed to be organized about it. So far, I hadn't gotten paid, so I could claim it was a hobby rather than a business. It beat knitting or golf, as far as I was concerned, but I couldn't count on people randomly showing up with problems, and if I was going to all this trouble, payment would be nice. That meant I had to figure out the rules for this kind of thing. What did it take to get a private investigator license? Did I need a business license too? Did PIs charge sales tax? Starting a business sounded like a lot of work.

Good thing I didn't have to tackle it alone.

I looked at my sister. "Set up a time next week for us to discuss our business partnership."

"Eeee!" She clapped her hands together and grinned like a little girl getting a pony on Christmas morning.

"Make a note to price sword canes for me," I said. What was the point of starting a business with your little sister if you couldn't boss her around? "Those really exist, right? If we're going to keep having nights like this, I might need one."

Jen gave a sharp nod and wrote in her notebook. "Sword canes. Got it."

Dad moaned softly. "Did I say I wanted you girls to get along again? What was I thinking?"

"Hey," I said, "if you didn't want us to tackle the world's problems, you shouldn't have raised us that way."

I'd gone into journalism in part out of a desire to save the world. That seemed naïve to me now. No matter how well you uncovered and reported the news, things seldom changed on a big scale. But this week, we'd saved one old man and caught a murderer. It wasn't world peace, but it was something.

For today, it was enough.

The End

Don't miss Kate Tessler's next adventure in
Someone Cruel in Coyote Creek!

Join Tule Publishing's newsletter for more great reads and weekly deals!

If you enjoyed *Something Deadly on Desert Drive*,
you'll love the next book in…

The Accidental Detective series

Book 1: *Something Shady at Sunshine Haven*

Book 2: *Something Deadly on Desert Drive*

Book 3: *Someone Cruel in Coyote Creek*
Coming in October 2022

Available now at your favorite online retailer!

About the Author

Kris Bock writes novels of mystery, suspense, and romance. She has lived in ten states and one foreign country but is now firmly planted in the Southwest, where many of her books are set. Her romantic suspense novels include stories of treasure hunting, archaeology, and intrigue. Readers have called these novels "Smart romance with an Indiana Jones feel." Learn more at www.krisbock.com or visit her Amazon page.

Kris's Furrever Friends Sweet Romance series features the employees and customers at a cat café. Watch as they fall in love with each other and shelter cats. Get a free 10,000-word story set in the world of the Furrever Friends cat café when you sign up for the Kris Bock newsletter.

Kris writes for children under the names Chris Eboch and M. M. Eboch. She has published over 60 books for young people, including ghostwriting for some famous mystery series. Her novels for ages nine and up include *Bandits Peak*, a survival thriller; *The Eyes of Pharaoh*, a mystery that brings ancient Egypt to life; and *The Well of Sacrifice*, an action-packed drama set in ninth-century Mayan Guatemala, used in many schools.

Kris lives in New Mexico, where she enjoys hiking, watching the sunset from her patio, and hanging out with her husband and their ferrets.

Thank you for reading

Something Deadly on Desert Drive

If you enjoyed this book, you can find more from all our great authors at TulePublishing.com, or from your favorite online retailer.

Printed in the USA
CPSIA information can be obtained
at www.ICGtesting.com
LVHW090413270624
784116LV00011BA/126